Donald Churchwell

TABLE OF CONTENTS

was about an hour after sundown, but the bright lights on the ramp revealed the smoke and the ground crew scurrying to pull wheel chocks. Their plane captain stood near the nose as James exercised all the control surfaces. The plane captain saluted them and headed for the warmth of the four-door blue pickup parked on the ramp with its engine running.

A scan of engine RPMs and exhaust temperatures appeared normal, and James keyed his mike. "Broadway Two Four taxi."

"Copy Two Four, taxi to runway Two Two and hold."

"Two Two and hold, Broadway copies." Toad glanced at his watch and turned to James. "Right on time, Major. Taxiing 2335 hrs, wheels up should be 2350."

James nodded. A Chrome Dome flight was an entirely different animal from an alert launch. During an alert launch, an entire flight of BUFFs would power up, elephant walk down the taxiway, and start their minimum interval takeoff routine with an aircraft releasing the brakes and rolling off every twelve seconds. In contrast, a Chrome Dome flight would usually be a solitary mission roughly twenty-four hours in duration. An eight-hour transit to a position near, but outside Soviet airspace, eight hours of orbiting inside a pre-arranged imaginary box, and an eight-hour transit home. The aircraft would meet a KC-135 tanker four times on this mission.

At any given time, there were other BUFFs performing the same mission around the perimeter of their Cold War enemy. Only some planner seated behind a desk at SAC headquarters knew the number of aircraft and their locations. It was rumored SAC Commander, General Curtis Lemay, selected the locations by throwing darts, but in truth, the aircraft crews had no idea how the selections were made.

Broadway Two Four taxied down the "Christmas Tree," rolling between dark, armed, alert aircraft. The contrast between the dark sky and the taxi lights seemed to make the white snow piled on the edges of the taxiway seem even brighter as Lt. Commander James peered through the windshield. Isolated flakes of snow appeared in the lights as the aircraft made the turn. They held off the end of the runway as instructed and immediately saw the reason for the hold as the lights of an incoming aircraft lit the darkened cockpit.

A minute later a tanker passed them on the way to its touchdown several hundred yards down the runway. The anti-collision lights on the tanker faded into the dark, snowy runway, and a few moments later, James heard the tower in his headphones.

"Broadway Two Four, you're cleared for takeoff."

Toad replied, "Copy Two Four is clear for takeoff."

The BUFF rolled onto the runway and stopped. The aircraft commander locked the brakes and brought the throttles up on the eight Pratt & Whitney J 57s. James and Toad carefully surveyed the gauges on a last check prior to rolling.

Major James reviewed the sheet on his knee board indicating the speeds the aircraft would use for last safe abort option and rotation speed based on their takeoff weight, wind speed, and temperature. S1 callout would tell the pilot flying the takeoff that the aircraft could not abort and must actually take off. S2 was the rotation speed, the point at which the aircraft's nose would be raised, and the BUFF would lumber into the air.

James and Toad confirmed the flaps were down and took one last look at the gauges telling them what was going on in the engines. James turned to Toad and told him, "You have the aircraft. Let's roll."

Toad nodded and released the brakes.

James keyed his mike and informed the tower, "Broadway Two Four is rolling."

"Copy Two Four rolling. Contact departure on 440.5. Have a good flight."

The B52 and its payload of four WA52 thermonuclear weapons lumbered down the runway, gradually accelerating to speed. Major James called off S1 and, seconds later, called off S2. Toad pulled up on the yoke, and the aircraft rotated, leaving the snow and Westover AFB behind, headed toward their objective some three thousand miles and two tankers away.

Chapter 2

Over the Barents Sea

0800 Zulu

James woke to the smell of coffee. Presently he was horizontal on an aluminum deck catching a nap. After some ten hours of flying, including a sunrise and two rendezvous with KC-135 tankers taking on sixty-thousand pounds of JP-5 aviation fuel each time, he had decided a nap would be appropriate.

Broadway Two Four was presently station keeping in a racetrack pattern several hundred miles long some two hundred miles off the northern coast of the USSR. Murmansk was the closest city of any size. This holding pattern would continue for eight hours. Assuming a "go code" was not sent to his aircraft, James and his crew would not turn south with their cargo of nuclear weapons to incinerate a target, or targets. The potential location of those targets was totally unknown to them until they opened sealed orders contained in a safe. Lacking the receipt of a "go code," they would simply turn and head for home.

Major James had been lying on the hard, check-plate deck for several hours in a semi-open part of the upper deck behind the pilot and copilot seats and in front of the rear-facing electronic warfare officer and the gunner. The headset kept his semi-conscious brain aware of mundane operational items, but any sign of alarm in the voices on the intercom would have awakened him instantly. He had slept, sort of, for a few hours. The odor of coffee being poured from someone's thermos, and the need to offload eight hours' worth of coffee he had consumed, roused him to a more awake than asleep mode.

He knew his copilot and a junior crew member were keeping things under control on the flight deck. For a strategic bomber, one element of the United States nuclear triad, the B-52 was actually a rather primitive mechanism to be trusted with the delivery of weapons that would incinerate a city of millions of souls.

The autopilot would sometimes disengage for no apparent reason. Near constant adjustments were needed to keep the aluminum tube airborne, not the least of which was moving fuel to maintain balance in the aircraft. The aircrew used a camp toilet if nature called, and the list of minor deficiencies was nearly endless.

James rose, stretching to attempt to relieve the pain in his back as he walked by the steep ladder down to the lower deck. The radar bombardier and navigator occupied seats on the lower level of the cockpit. In a B-52, the arrangement meant that the lower deck crews' ejection seats fired down, through the floor, while everyone on the upper deck ejected up, through the bomber's roof. Any catastrophe requiring ejection at low altitudes could potentially be a death sentence for the lower deck crew.

As the aircraft commander, that fact was always in the back of his mind. On this particular mission, another fact was that the water temperatures they were flying over ran just a degree or two above freezing. That meant that any ejection, regardless of altitude, would mean the crew's life expectancy once they reached the ocean could be measured in minutes, at a maximum.

James made his way to the aircraft commander's seat, tapping Lt. Ayers on the shoulder. He shouted, "Thanks for the chance for a nap. I'm back."

Taking his seat, he asked his copilot, "Feeling okay, Toad? Did you get any sleep on your break?"

"Yessir, doing okay. Looks like we only have another couple hours before we take her to the barn."

"Agreed. Let's hope it's a quiet two hours."

"Roger that."

James got on the intercom and polled his crew, checking on them. He had a good crew. No superstars, but no troublemakers either. Unit cohesion was important. An aircrew didn't have to be outstanding to a man, but one asshole could make a mission much more difficult than it already was.

He thought it was probably a normal feeling, but the majority of the time he could almost imagine he was commanding a cargo plane or airliner. The fact that there were four metal cylinders twenty feet behind him, each of which could turn a city into a smoking pile of cinders just like Hiroshima, didn't seem real.

The bombs were an abstraction. When forced to consider it, he saw himself and his crew as peacekeepers. As long as the United States and the Soviet Union each had the ability to turn each other to radioactive rubble, there should theoretically be no desire to be the first one to pull the trigger. The concept of Mutually Assured Destruction had kept the peace for twenty some years now, conflicts like Korea notwithstanding.

They were presently flying in daylight about six miles above a cloud deck. Beneath the clouds was the gray, choppy, nearly frozen surface of the Barents Sea. To the north was the Arctic Circle, to the west, Finland, Sweden, and Norway. At these northern latitudes, the daylight had a strange, low-sun angle requiring him to keep the dark helmet visor down. Then there was the fact that daylight itself was a condition that only lasted about three hours per day. He actually preferred flying at night because he could see the backlit instruments better.

He was mentally reviewing their upcoming rendezvous with the first KC-135 tanker they would meet on the way home. It would be dark again by then. Tanking at night was tricky. As long as the level of midair turbulence was low, and as long as he and the airman flying the boom that actually delivered the fuel to the thirsty bomber did their jobs, it would be a routine operation that only made his palms sweat a little.

The task of placing a tanker orbiting in exactly the right location at exactly the right time Broadway Two Four arrived was simpler than it seemed, but still a minor source of amazement to James. Since the B-52 was under total radio and emission silence, they would have their radar off. Once they were within ten miles or so, he should be able to see the tanker's anti-collision lights. At that point, they could make contact on their UHF radios. The very short range on these radios would prevent any prying ears from picking them up, unless they were close as well.

James knew the approach would be made using guidance lights on the tanker and directions for final approach and hook-up to the fueling boom. The boom would be directed, literally flown, by the operator in the KC-135. Once attached, fuel would flow from the tanker to the BUFF at a rate of up to 1,000 gallons per minute, or about 6,500 pounds per minute in aircraft jargon. James would fly the fueling run as Toad passed the fuel to the proper internal tanks on the bomber. The changes in weight as the B-52 took on added weight would cause slight changes in the flight characteristics that only experience compensated for.

The entire process was a routine, and dangerous, ballet between two heavy jets taking place seven miles above a cold, dark sea. Without that dance, Broadway Two Four would never get home. There were alternate landing sites in the U.K. or Greenland at military bases. Other options were available, but only as a last resort. SAC frowned on a loaded B-52 setting down anywhere that was unprepared and unequipped to secure the plane, and its weapons. No aircraft commander would want an incident like that in his jacket.

James was in a strange zone right now. He was awake, but he had no doubts that there were moments, maybe seconds or even minutes, that he might be technically asleep. He was probably in one of those zones when his navigator, Lt. Fred Stone, roused him. "Major, time's up. Our turn in the box is done."

"Copy, Flint. How about a vector and distance to the gas pump?" With a name like Fred Stone, the navigator's entire career would be full of references to the popular cartoon character. Hardly a day went by that Fred's wife wasn't referred to as Wilma.

"Roger, two-seven-two degrees, roughly four hundred nautical miles, sir."

"Copy that. Aircraft commander to crew, be advised our shift is over, headed back to the barn. The Ruskies are safe for today." A minor feeling of relief passed through James' brain. There would be no need for his crew's professional services today, and that was a good thing.

Chapter 3

One hour after refueling

Major James glanced at his watch. It had been roughly an hour since Broadway Two Four had tanked. He knew that would put them roughly an hour away from Greenland. Thule Air Force Base in Greenland was the first location telling an inbound aircraft like his that home, the U.S., was close by. James always had a sense that Greenland marked the "hump." He could feel the mission was truly on the downhill run once they passed Greenland and that every minute that passed placed the crew eight miles closer to their homes and families.

The first clue there could be a problem came as might be expected, from the instruments. Every pilot, regardless of whether his aircraft was a Cessna 172 or a B-52, had a system of scanning the instruments. He, or she, would have an instinctive knowledge of what the many dials *should* say. Not so much the actual values as much as the position of the needle in its place on the dial. During the Second World War, when aircraft made huge changes in complexity, many pilots would have their plane captain physically rotate the actual gauge so that in "normal" conditions, the needle pointed straight up. In that way a quick scan of the instrument panel would show a needle that wasn't vertical. That gauge would receive instant attention.

James' present scan noted small movements in the voltage on one of the primary busses. That wasn't normal.

"Smoke in the lower bay!" That was navigator Flint's voice, and that *definitely* wasn't normal. A moment later, most of the gauges on the instrument panel went dark and a garbled voice came through the failing intercom yelling, "Fire!"

James motioned to his copilot to go below and help. He then buckled his oxygen mask over his face. He could already smell the acrid stench wafting up to the flight deck. This was serious, really, really screwed-up shit. He flipped a lever to depressurize the cabin, hoping his crew had the foresight to have gone on oxygen as well. That was well established protocol and drilled into the crew as the first step to take in the event of a cabin fire.

Venting the cabin would carry off some of the smoke and also reduce the amount of oxygen available to a fire. He knew the crew would be using CO_2 extinguishers in the area of the fire. The problem was that the busses, large conductors of power for the aircraft, were behind covers and, for the most part, totally inaccessible.

He pulled out a flashlight and scanned his panel to see what he still had. Compass, check. Altimeter, check. Artificial horizon and airspeed, check. That seemed to be about it.

James pushed the yoke down slightly and put the aircraft into a shallow dive. He still had engines and hydraulics, so he could fly. Sort of. By memory he knew they were over one hundred miles from Greenland. Could he find Thule and its runway with basically no instruments? He had no idea, but that was the only option that held a remotely satisfactory ending to the mission.

He tried his radio, and, as expected, it was dead. Broadway Two Four was supposed to still be under radio silence, but for the sake of his crew, he would have been willing to put out a Mayday on the VHF radio. Since the radios were dead, that wasn't an option. Watching the altimeter, he saw the aircraft was passing through twelve thousand feet. He pulled his mask off. The smoke and stench had decreased quite a bit thankfully.

Three or so minutes later, Toad re-appeared and took his place in the co-pilot seat. James yelled to him, "What's the verdict?"

"Fire's out, for now, but as you can probably tell, we have no power. As I see it, we're fucked, sir."

James nodded. "Maybe so, yes. I suppose there's no chance of a fix unless you know something I don't."

"No, sir. What are you thinking?"

"Bailing out is not an option. We'd be dead within three minutes of hitting the water. My plan, shitty as it is, is to try to make Thule, or anything resembling hard ground in the vicinity of Thule."

"Agreed. How far out do you think we are? And what do we have?"

James pulled his flashlight out again, looking at the instruments. "I have no fucking idea what's working and what isn't. We have eight good engines and hydraulics right now. Nothing that takes electrical power. Look in the manual and see if there's anything close to this situation in it." James knew the manual by heart and knew Toad would find nothing. On the other hand, it would keep Toad busy, and maybe he would see something James had failed to see or remember.

James panned his few active gauges again. Broadway Two Four was passing through ten thousand feet. He eased up on the yoke to level out. He could see he was still on a compass course for Greenland, and a runway. He felt a tap on his shoulder. It was Flint from the lower deck.

"Sir, what should I tell the guys downstairs?"

"Tell them we're in pretty deep shit, but the plan is to try to limp to Thule, or anything that looks like hard ground. There's no point in punching out. That's suicide. Go talk to them and then come back. I hope to tell them something soon. You can relay for us, okay?"

Flint nodded and gave James a look that said he understood and headed for the ladder to the lower deck.

The pilot turned to his co-pilot. "Toad, can you see if there's a way to kill the emergency lighting up here and get me landing lights?"

"Yessir, I'll work on it."

Several minutes later, Toad turned to James. "Sir, I think I might be able to run a jumper to the landing lights. According to the schematic, there's no way to kill the emergency lights with a breaker. Separate battery, separate circuit."

"Okay, plan on taking off the covers and breaking the bulbs up here in the cockpit. When I have to put this thing down, I need some night vision."

Toad didn't reply. He simply nodded.

James fumed internally. This shit wasn't supposed to happen. It was one thing to lose an aircraft because you had been shot down by enemy forces or because, as a pilot, you had committed some mortal sin, but to be downed by a mechanical failure over hostile conditions just seemed unfair somehow. He had often talked to fighter pilots over large quantities of adult beverages. Fighter pilots had a credo that went something like "God, please don't let me fuck up, but if I do, don't let me fuck up and live." He understood the theory behind the quote, but fighter pilots flew a tube of aluminum that contained only themselves, not a crew of six.

Toad re-appeared. "Major, try the landing lights."

James did so, and they worked. "Good work. That gives us a chance. Ask Flint if he has a guess for a vector and distance to Thule please. And grab a PRC 90 out of a bailout kit and see if we can contact anyone on it."

Toad cracked a small smile. "Okay, good idea, sir. I'll be back in a few."

James looked at his watch. His mental estimate was that they were less than one hundred fifty miles from Greenland. Thule would be quite a bit farther, but at this point, a runway was a runway., and terra firma of any kind was better than an ice-water grave.

Something felt wrong, as if there wasn't already enough going on to ruin his day. James could feel a slight yaw in the flight characteristics; his plane was pulling to the left. If he had instruments, he knew he would see one of the four engines on the left wing was either way down on power or not running at all. He could see a small decrease in airspeed on the gauge. It was still working because air pressure drove the gauge by mechanical means. No power needed. "Toad, I'm losing power. Any ideas on why?"

"Yeah, we should have changed tanks a while ago."

"Which requires power, which means we're going to lose power completely in minutes, right?"

Toad nodded. "Yep, afraid so, sir. Time to earn our pay with some fancy pilot shit, sir."

James turned his flashlight to Toad's face. His copilot had just told him they were all going to die, and he was grinning. James shook his head and pushed the yoke down again. No reason to run out of fuel two miles up. Better to get closer to the deck, under the clouds, and see what was there. Maybe he was wrong about their position. Maybe Broadway Two Four would sprout wings and fly back to Westover.

Chapter 4

One hundred miles off Greenland
Altitude 1,500 feet

Broadway Two Four was now under the cloud deck and making four hundred fifty knots. Major James guestimated they were running on four of their eight engines. The aircraft was in a seriously ugly situation, running out of fuel, without power, and who knows how far from solid ground. It really didn't get much worse than this, James thought, unless you had just been hit by a ground-to-air missile and the aircraft was in multiple pieces.

Thanks to some ingenious jury-rigging on his copilot's part, he had landing lights, at least. Unfortunately, right now all the lights revealed was dark, and incredibly cold, salt water. The cockpit was quiet. His copilot had no brilliant suggestions, no surprise there, and the intercom was quiet since they had no power. James realized it was all on him. He had no tricks up his sleeves, so in his opinion, the most likely outcome at this point was that all of them were going to die.

They could bail out, but that would result in a matter of minutes before they hit the water and then a minute, maybe two, until they succumbed to hypothermia and died. The radios on the aircraft were dead. At James's suggestion, the copilot had pulled a radio from a bailout pack with a limited range and was issuing Mayday calls, but to no avail so far.

In the northern darkness, James' field of vision was limited to what the landing lights and his eyes could discern, maybe a mile or two. All he had seen for the last ten minutes consisted of black water and occasional ice floes. As he willed his eyes to see farther and farther away, he thought he saw a wall of white. He looked away for a moment and panned his flashlight over the instrument panel. Airspeed was dropping again. Another engine had starved for fuel apparently.

Turning off the flashlight, he waited a few seconds to let his eyes adjust to the darkness ahead. There was no doubt; a wall of white was there at the limits of his vision. Was it Greenland? Doubtful, at least according to his sense of position based on the last reliable information he had processed, but could it be a place to put Broadway Two Four down?

James turned to his copilot and hit him in the shoulder. "Be ready to put this thing down, Toad. I don't know if what I'm seeing is Greenland or an ice floe, but I may be making a decision in the next few minutes."

Toad looked at his commander. For a moment, James saw panic in his copilot's eyes, followed by resignation and understanding. "Roger that. Do we want the gear down?"

Was he serious? "Negative, I don't see any concrete, do you?"

Toad showed weak grin. "Gotcha, sir, dumb-ass question, sorry."

"Unbuckle, and tell everyone to prepare for a rough landing. Tell them to buckle up and be ready to exit the aircraft ASAP. Oh, tell them to safe the weapons if it can be done without power."

Toad nodded and proceeded to leave his seat. James looked out the windscreen again. The white he thought he had seen was getting closer by the second, and there was no black water behind it, yet. His mind was made up. Right or wrong, the flight was ending here and now. He knocked all eight throttle levers down to about half-throttle since he had no clue which engines were still operating.

The white wall grew closer. His view of it lacked any real details because of the poor lighting. He could see there were no obvious mountains, but it was impossible to tell if he was looking at a relatively smooth surface or a frozen version of Hell on earth. He decided the best landing technique would be similar to what he had heard his fellow B-52 pilots discuss for a water landing. Slow and low, and then at a point just barely above stall speed, and about forty feet up, easing the nose up for a deliberate stall with the tail hitting first.

Truth be told, without a long, hard-surfaced runway, putting a BUFF down was a crash, not a landing. James considered his options one more time.

Toad showed up, standing at his side. James turned to him with an afterthought. "One more thing,

Toad. Tell everyone we need to exit from the upper deck escape hatches because, as soon as I see something that looks half-assed flat, I'm putting her down." The escape hatches were the same hull openings that the ejection seats fired through. Each hatch had about six latches that had to be opened to use it as an exit.

James was happy to see Toad returning to his seat and buckling up just as Broadway Two Four flashed over the edge of the ice. "Any thoughts, Toad? Unfiltered, just say what you feel."

"Well, sir, it looks kinda rough. Looks like a mix of ice and powder. Be nice if it was all powder. Got any feel for the real distance to the surface?"

"Nope. Been looking at the shadows from the landing lights and making guesses. Also, I've got no idea which way the winds are out of. My idea is to get the flaps down, trim her up, and start a slow circle to see if I can feel any advantage with a particular heading. Gimme the flaps and I'll start. Break out the binoculars and tell me if you see a spot you'd like to call a runway."

"Gotcha."

"Oh, I'm assuming Flint isn't getting anything on the PRC 90."

"Nope. Flaps feel like they're down, working on trim."

"Shit!" James let fly. The aircraft was crabbing again. Another engine had flamed out. Broadway Two Four was starving for fuel. It was now or never. He increased the throttles on all the port engines, hoping he could take the crab out.

The flaps had dragged the plane down to about two hundred twenty knots. Slightly above stall speed. He lumbered the crippled bomber toward an area that looked as flat as any about a half-mile out. "Hit the master alarm. I'm putting her down."

Toad nodded and hit the alarm. It would signal the crew to assume crash position, had it worked. With no electricity, of course it didn't.

James pointed the nose down, levelling out at what looked like about one hundred feet. He pulled all the throttles back to just above idle and let the nose dip all on its own. As the white, icy surface came up, he slowly pulled back on the yoke.

Broadway Two Four shuddered into a mild stall that migrated into the real thing at something just over one hundred knots. It felt like the tail hit first as the four-hundred-thousand-pound aluminum tube hit the ice.

James felt a huge shock as the fuselage pounded into the white surface, followed by obscene grating noises as the belly of the plane skidded across the ice/snow mix. He couldn't see the wings, but he could feel the plane yaw from side to side as parts of the engines or wings, or both, were ripped away. He silently prayed nothing would tear the wings completely off and allow the fuselage to roll. That would likely remove any chances of the crew surviving.

A reddish-orange glow from the port side windows signaled a fire of some sort in that wing. The engines might be starved for fuel, but there was still fuel in some of the tanks; they just couldn't access those tanks without power to operate the valves. The aircraft seemed to hop a little as it crossed a bump, and then suddenly all he could see ahead was the white of a solid bank of snow or ice. Broadway Two Four piled into the bank. James was thrown forward in his straps. His head hit the dash, and his world went dark.

As consciousness slowly returned, Major James began to collect information from his surroundings. At first he thought it was deathly silent, but then he realized it was not that quiet at all. It was simply the absence of the pervasive whine of the jet engines. No, it was far from quiet. He could hear cracks and creaks. The total darkness of the cockpit amplified his sense of sound.

"Toad." He turned to his right, searching for his flashlight. Hearing no response, he felt toward his co-pilot and felt, snow?

As his eyed slowly adapted, it appeared the windscreen had breached on Toad's side. He pulled off his glove and reached for Toad's neck. His hand was stopped by a jagged piece of ice or windshield. His copilot and friend was quite dead; his head was almost separated from his body.

The noise level ratcheted up, or at least his perception of it increased. Cracks and crunches, accompanied by the sound of shredding metal, and now, movement? How could the plane be moving? It suddenly came to him. They were not in Greenland. They were short of the land mass by God knows how much. He had landed on a huge ice floe, and the ice couldn't bear the weight of a nearly half-million-pound metal object. He, his aircraft, and his crew were sinking. He had lost everything, his aircraft, his crew, and now his life.

He said a silent prayer to God to protect his family and to accept his soul. The icy-cold, black water touched his booted feet. It should be over in just a few more minutes. He bowed his head and cried. No one would ever know.

Chapter 5

Strategic Air Command Headquarters

Offutt Air Force Base

Omaha, Nebraska. 1700 hrs local time

Colonel Martin Parks sat at his desk at the top level of a smallish, darkened amphitheater. Huge projector screens at one end of the room showed multiple world maps with the locations of United States and Soviet air assets. Projected charts down the left and right sides of the display showed how many nuclear strike bombers and intercontinental missile were available and their respective states of readiness.

The country's strategic air assets were currently at DEFCON Four, one step from the lowest threat level. Parks gazed down on the amphitheater, looking over twenty-odd men at their stations, each with their own displays. A haze of blueish cigarette smoke hung in the dark, seventy-two-degree air, along with the smell of a coffee pot that had been allowed to cook coffee rather than warm it, and the faint hint of pizza.

Something on the display at the end of the room caught his eye. A flashing triangle appeared near Greenland. Before he could even get terribly curious, the black telephone built into his console showed a flashing amber light under it. *Better than the red phone!* He picked it up. "Parks."

"Colonel, it's Abrahams, Chrome Dome."

Parks knew Abrahams well. He was a lieutenant colonel, the supervisor for all Chrome Dome flights during his duty watch. Under the present DEFCON conditions, he was probably the de-facto second-in-command in the room. Parks was the senior officer. Under him were officers that supervised Chrome Dome, Alert Forces, and Missiles. Until the DEFCON status advanced to a high threat situation, the Chrome Dome B-52s with their nuclear cargos were the most important aircraft SAC managed.

"Yes?" Parks answered.

"Sir, we have a situation here. Broadway Two Four was inbound from their turn in the box. They made their first tanker as scheduled, but were a no-show at the second rendezvous."

"Any radio call, indications of a crash?"

"Negative, sir. In theory, if they were following their flight plan, they should have been over water."

"Any indication of any Ruskie air or naval assets in the general area?"

"No, sir. We're tracking a Soviet Bear bomber on what looks like a routine training mission several hundred miles south of Broadway's intended course. No naval activity we know about anywhere close."

"Theoretically when would they be out of fuel?"

"About thirty minutes, sir."

"Home base?"

"Westover."

"Okay. I need a crew list, aircraft file, and serial numbers on the payload. Contact the C.O. at Westover, give him a brief, and tell him to be standing by."

"Yes, sir."

"One more thing. Who's the aircraft commander?"

"A Major David James, sir."

"Very well. Get busy, Colonel."

"Yes, sir."

Parks hung his phone up. He knew James; he had flown with him. It put a personal sense of loss spin to the situation. He had a potential Broken Arrow on his hands. In about ten minutes, he would be briefing General Curtis Lemay, SAC commander, that a U.S. Air Force B-52 carrying nuclear weapons was down somewhere in the North Atlantic. Lemay would be unhappy, putting it mildly. A Broken Arrow was about as bad as it got. It was SAC terminology for nuclear weapons being missing. This briefing was going to suck.

Offutt secure briefing room
Thirty minutes later

Lemay leaned back in his large leather chair. He removed the fat cigar from his mouth; it had gone out some time ago. He put the cigar in his cut-glass ashtray and looked around the room at the four senior officers and three staff lieutenants seated at the table. The brief had been short. Lemay had listened and thumbed through the files in front of him without asking a single question or issuing anything resembling an order, until now. "Gentlemen, this entire discussion does not leave this room." He spent several minutes re-lighting his cigar. "Go ahead and have the C.O. at Westover assemble a group of officers to visit the families. The families are to be informed the men are overdue and missing from a training mission. Initiate a search, military assets only. A B-52 out of Westover on a routine training mission is missing."

"Sir?" Parks blurted out. "Training mission? Sir, this is a Chrome Dome mission. We're in a Broken Arrow situation."

Lemay blew smoke toward Parks. "Colonel, the waters off Greenland are deep and cold. Unless and until we find this aircraft, we don't have a Broken Arrow unless I say we do." He looked around the room, staring into each man's eyes, gauging their response. "Are there any questions?"

The young lieutenant in charge of public affairs cleared his throat. "Press release, General Lemay?"

"Have Westover release the loss of the plane in the morning. They will not issue anything until all the families have been personally informed."

Parks glared at Lemay. "What about the weapons inventory, *sir*?"

"That's not your concern, Colonel; it's mine. You would do well to remember that." He sat for a moment or two. "Dismissed!" Lemay watched the men file out of the room. Parks hesitated for a moment, staring at Lemay. Then he shook his head and followed the others out, closing the door behind him.

Lemay pondered his position. As the highest ranking active commander in the Air Force, he was still subject to political pressure from the Joint Chiefs to the Secretary of Defense and, ultimately, the White House. His actions were improper, possibly even illegal, but necessary. He had no need for a Broken Arrow right now. Nothing that he could do would bring Broadway Two Four or its crew or the four bombs back. Hopefully they were all lying in a deep, dark, and cold grave. In a few weeks, everything would return to normal.

The aircraft, its crew, and its lethal cargo would have been replaced. A year from now, the aircraft would be nothing but a memory to the crew's family and friends. He felt a sense of loss, but no regrets.

Chapter 6

September 7, 2003

Onboard United Flight 92

Enroute Heathrow to New York

Fakhir Arafat peered out the Plexiglas window one more time. The view hadn't changed. All he saw was dark water with scattered clouds. He thought back. Had he been chosen for this mission for his name? In Arabic, Fakhir stood for pride and excellence. Or was it because he was a distant relative of Yasser Arafat, leader of the Palestinian people?

Fakhir was only twenty-two. He already held the rank of captain with the PLO. He'd volunteered for his mission. As he looked around the cabin, he found it amusing that his fellow passengers would feel differently about him if they could see him in his normal attire.

As a captain in the PLO, he normally wore olive drab, wore a keffiyah over his head, and carried an AK-47. Today he wore a suit, a white dress shirt, open at the collar, and carried a modified garage door opener along with his car keys. Security in London had regarded him with suspicion. They had even searched his luggage a second time. Little did they know he would be meeting his explosives onboard.

A new Hewlet-Packard printer was supposed to be somewhere in the cargo hold. It had been modified by PLO explosives experts in Italy and loaded on the Boeing 747 in Milan as cargo earlier in the day. Fakhir's instructions had been to trigger the left button on the garage door opener to confirm communication with the printer. Once that was done, his mission was a "go." A failure of communication would mean that he simply rode to New York as a passenger. The mission could be attempted at another time.

As it happened, pushing the left button on the garage door opener had resulted in the small L.E.D. on the opener flashing three times, indicating the opener was communicating with the printer.

Pressing the right button on the opener for ten seconds would initiate the detonation sequence, triggering nearly a kilo of Semtex. Fakhir was not privy to where the powerful explosive had come from, nor the design of the bomb, only the intended result.

The aftermath would be to bring down a U.S. flag airliner with hundreds of infidels, and hopefully as many Jews as possible, in the deep, cold waters off Greenland. The PLO would take credit for the bombing, and pressure would be applied to the West in hopes of acknowledgement of the State of Palestine. Fakhir would join Allah and be rewarded with seventy-two virgins in the afterlife. Additionally, in earthly terms, his family would receive financial rewards from the PLO.

Fakhir looked at his watch again. His instructions were very specific. The bomb needed to be triggered two hours after takeoff from Heathrow to put the aircraft wreckage in the ideal position. The depth of the North Atlantic in that location would theoretically make it nearly impossible to reach. Ten minutes remained.

He looked around the cabin one more time. To his left, two Englishmen in suits. Obviously businessmen of some sort. An American family sat in the row ahead of him, a mother, father, and a cute, young, blonde daughter. The family spoke in animated terms of their vacation in London. Several rows ahead, an American group of high school students sat, laughing and joking about their European tour. The infidels disgusted him. They enjoyed drugs, sex; they were abominations. His mission would remove them from this life. The next life would be their problem; his afterlife was assured.

Fakhir glanced once more at his watch. It was time. Fishing the opener from his pocket, he held it in his hand. Unbuckling his seat belt, he stood and pressed the right button, holding it down firmly. After three or four seconds, he stood and yelled, "Allah Akbar."

Somewhere under the first class section, the final contacts closed inside the printer, detonating the Semtex. The blast blew out the bottom of the Boeing 747. The rapid, massive decompression of the cargo bay caused the floor of the passenger compartment to collapse, literally tearing the nose of the aircraft away. The remainder of the Boeing passenger compartment instantly decompressed and allowed a blast of seventy-degrees-below-zero air to pass through the cabin.

A few passengers seated immediately over the bomb died instantly. The remainder of the cabin, Fakhir included, lived another few moments as the five-hundred-mile-per-hour blast of icy air shredded the fragile protoplasm of flesh and humanity a second or two later. A few people near the tail might have actually survived for another half-minute or so until decompression and lack of oxygen rendered them unconscious.

A scant three minutes later, the first pieces of Flight 92 impacted the icy-cold waters of the North Atlantic enroute to their resting place on the abyssal plain, some two miles below the surface. Within twenty minutes, United Flight 92 existed in two forms; light items, capable of floating, began to dissipate across the surface, directed by winds and currents, and heavier items, finding homes on the bottom of the North Atlantic.

Chapter 7

Michael James MacAdams was known as to his friends as "Mac." Okay, "friends" might be something of an overstatement in his case. He didn't have many. Perhaps it was due to the fact that in an organization like Woods Hole, a place occupied by men and women with initials after their names and bright-eyed grad students, he was the guy that had to say "No."

Woods Hole had become world famous after the discovery of the *Titanic*, the *Bismarck*, the *Lusitania* and others. Donations and TV offers poured in. Unfortunately, so did requests from legitimate sources, and nut cases as well, to take up their investigation. Their resources were not endless, and the directors looked to MacAdams to help select the projects that would actually be worth taking on, as well as the ships and crews to staff them.

In Mac's case, he actually had a little time to breathe right now. While mission planning, equipping their ships, and assorted logistics normally involved a minimum three-month lead time, this was break time for him. The Atlantic season for exploration was closing due to customary shitty weather and seas.

It was time for the ships to undergo annual maintenance. His crews were headed out for vacations, and grad students would be headed back to their respective campuses with stories of their trips and summer romances on the high seas.

Mac rose from his chair, standing to his full six-feet-four height, and limped down the hall from his terminally unorganized office to the coffee pot. Maddie, his assistant for the last four years, made a pot every four hours, assuming he hadn't finished it off sooner. He never asked her to fetch coffee for him; it had always somehow felt wrong. Mac had fallen into an ideal retirement job. Being a dive master for the Navy had prepared him well.

Not actually having attended SEAL BUD/S school hadn't stopped him from training with the squids, supporting them, and actually taking part in a few missions. Retirement from the Navy as a Senior Chief at age forty-five hadn't worked out well. A few years in the world of civilian commercial diving had led him accidently to this job at Woods Hole managing the operational side of exploring ocean bottoms all over the world.

He returned to his desk and sat down, lifting his legs to throw his cowboy boots on his desk. He opened his desk drawer and pulled out the latest Clive Cussler book. Cussler was his favorite reading, other than non-fiction related to his line of work. His home library held at least a thousand books, counting paperbacks. His favorites were non-fiction, but Cussler's books were simplistic, fun reads.

He had no sooner reached a comfortable position, back pain aside, when his desk phone rang. He could see from the display that the director was calling. This was seldom a good sign. "MacAdams. How can I help you, Dr. Thomas?"

"Hello, Mac. How's your day going?"

"Nothing has gone wrong yet, sir, but might I assume that's about to change?"

"Mac, that's a somewhat pessimistic attitude, wouldn't you agree?"

"Of course, Director. How can I help you?"

"Been watching TV lately?"

"No, sir, I try my best to avoid it."

"Hmm, yes, I'd heard that about you. Anyway, two days ago, a U.S. flag airliner went down somewhere between Iceland and Greenland. The PLO has taken credit. The FAA, the NTSB, and, most importantly, the State Department and the President's Chief of Staff want to find the wreckage and retrieve the black boxes."

"You do know they're orange, don't you?"

"Interesting, no, I didn't, but that's unimportant at this point. What I need, what Woods Hole needs, is to put a ship to sea immediately set up to hunt the aircraft. What would that involve, in your opinion?"

MacAdams considered the task in his head. "First thing, sir, how accurate is the position information we have?"

"Unsure, I can certainly check on that. While I'm investigating that, is there anything else you need to know?"

"Well, yes, there is actually. I need to know what our mission would be. Finding the wreckage dictates one part of the mission, but recovering anything from the wreckage will require an entirely different set of assets. A whole other ship, equipment, people with different skills."

"Okay, I can see that."

"One more thing, Director. Can you see if the government intends to involve DOD?"

"I'm sure you have a good reason, but why would we need the Defense Department?"

"If we could involve the Navy, they could check their hydrophone system and possibly find the sound of impact when something that large hit the surface. Second, any Navy sub in the general area could possibly hear the pings from the black boxes. Those assets could narrow the search area by a bunch."

"Thanks, Mac. Very good information, and I'll get busy on my end. At this point, start putting a mission plan together and a boat and crew for location."

MacAdams leaned back in his chair. A ship and crew would be difficult, but not impossible; hell, he could captain the vessel if need be. The techies would be a challenge too. With the grad students unavailable, he would have to begin trying to locate technicians.

Side-scan sonar, towed sonar array, towed video, all would require highly skilled deck operators on the winches and skilled interpreters on the ship.

A horrible thought came to him. It was almost a certainty he would need that asshole Blackie. John fucking Black. The most skilled and widely hated principle investigator in the business. PhD., former Navy sub officer, former SEAL team member, and a certifiably crazy alcoholic. His team hated his guts. Mac hated his guts. But when you needed results, you just bit the bullet and called the man. That was what he would do. Clive Cussler would have to wait.

Chapter 8

The Bluejacket Bar
Washington, D.C.

"Blackie, your jacket's beeping."

John Black looked up from a tricky bank shot on the pool table. He picked up his cigarette from its resting place on the side of the table. Taking a long drag, he rolled his eyes and walked to the table where he and his newfound friends were seated.

He pulled the pager from an inside pocket in his worn, leather Navy SEAL jacket. Actually, the jacket didn't actually "say" anything about being a SEAL. His name and rank were on the right breast, and the gold wings, trident, and anchor embroidered in gold on the left breast identified Black as a SEAL to anyone who recognized the emblem. Looking at the pager, he instantly recognized the number.

"Fucking Mac," he growled, almost under his breath. "Guys, I'm out of this game for a while. Gotta call home." Black finished his vodka tonic, put on his jacket, and walked out of the dimly lit, smoky bar into the late afternoon September sun. He could see the Washington Navy Yard a few blocks away. He felt the hint of early fall in the air.

He pulled a BlackBerry out of his jacket and powered it up.

Thinking back, he recalled what a page had meant when he was attached to a SEAL team. Report for duty within an hour, regardless of where you were or what condition you were in. He had loved his stint with the SEALs, even though it had cost him a marriage and, eventually, his career. Being a sub weapons officer had been interesting, but oddly unfulfilling. A Ph.D. in nuclear physics resulted in easy entry to the Navy. His wife had been less than enthused at the time, but the status of being a naval officer's wife had actually pleased her more than his high salaried job with General Dynamics.

Being associated with a SEAL team attached to his sub had appealed to his sense of wanderlust and excitement beyond his ability to resist. It had taken one waiver after another to even let him into BUD/S class because of his rank and value as a prisoner if captured. John Black's age had prevented his successful completion of BUD/S. But rather than ringing the bell and quitting, he had been silently removed in the middle of the night and assigned to a SEAL team on the East Coast under circumstances well disguised by the Navy office of personnel.

His position with the team had been tailored to his areas of expertise. Specifically, he wound up accompanying SEAL teams on missions that potentially involved "dirty bombs." The team he was on had intercepted the movement of nuclear material by known terrorists. The team had also participated in surreptitious entries into countries pursuing building nuclear weapons in several locations across the globe. Black knew what to look for and how to sabotage the process going on in whatever secret lab they penetrated.

The press never had any clue what the team had done. That was how they worked. The only way the media, or the public for that matter, would ever know anything about their missions would be if they had failed.

He had experienced two personal failures during his stint with the specialized SEAL team. The first had been a catastrophic end to his marriage for many reasons, mostly errors in judgment on his part. The second had been a mission that should have been viewed as a success by an outside observer, but his commanders, and some of his team, felt differently. Blackie had refused to concede they were right, and he and the Navy had agreed to part ways.

A year or two later, Woods Hole became his new home, and now those bastards, or specifically that bastard Mac, was summoning him when he was supposed to be on leave.

Dialing the number on the pager, he waited for an answer.

"Blackie?"

"What's up, Mac? You do realize I'm on leave, and rather intoxicated as well."

"I should consider this as a recent development, John?"

"Fuck you. You and I both know you're only calling me as a last resort, am I wrong?"

"Of course not. You're absolutely correct, as usual. Tactful as well. Bottom line, how soon can you be back at Woods Hole?"

"Well, I suppose once I sober up, I can drive up there. Say, sometime tomorrow?"

"No, John, now. This is important. Pay your tab, call a cab, and get on the Amtrak. Let me know your arrival time and someone will pick you up."

"I'm not hunting some rotting wreck, am I?"

"No, you're not. It's important. I can't discuss it on this line, but if you've looked at a paper in the last two days, I think you'll figure it out."

"Right, okay then. I'll call when I have an ETA. Adios." Black pushed the end button on his BlackBerry and powered it down. For him, cell phones were useful for placing calls. Being tethered to some gadget that others could use to summon *you* did not compute in his world. Following that reasoning, the BlackBerry he held could normally be found powered off. That damned Mac. Black hated his guts. His reasons would make no sense to most rational people. He hated Mac because he was everything Black was not. Mac was methodical, cunning even. He achieved what he wanted by persuasion, logic, and making others believe his suggestions were the other person's own idea.

Black, on the other hand, accomplished his ends by threats, coercion, blackmail, and lots and lots of cursing. In combat, miles behind enemy lines or four hundred meters below the surface trailing a Russian ballistic missile sub, there was no place for tact. A pretty good decision made quickly almost always trumped a great decision made too late.

Black shook his head, silently cursed Mac, and walked back into the bar. He walked to the bar, tossed a fifty on the counter, and growled, "Give me a to-go cup and call me a fuckin cab, Angel."

The tall, redheaded bartender with the rack shoved up into the scooped neck of her tee shirt smiled. "Had enough, Blackie?" she asked as she poured Stoli and some ice into a plastic cup. Placing it inside another plastic cup, with a bar napkin between the cups as an insulator, she smiled at him.

"No, beautiful, nowhere close, but duty calls. Somebody's gotta be a hero."

"Right." She pushed a wad of ones toward him, which he shoved back. "Later tonight? Shift change is in a few hours. Maybe you and me...?" She grinned coyly.

"Nah, baby. Rain check?"

"Anything for a big tipper. I'll call your cab." She turned and walked to the other end of the bar.

Black stared at the view lecherously. He smiled and walked outside. Should be enough time to finish his sixth drink for the afternoon and smoke one or two more before the cab arrived. He'd have to dry out on the train. Thank God the no-smoking policy at Woods Hole didn't apply offshore.

While he stood on the curb, he looked down the street. He saw a newspaper vending machine. Walking down to it, he shoved two quarters in and pulled out a *Washington Post. Holy shit!* Mac was right. Right there, front page, below the fold. *Search continues for debris from United Airlines 747 with 248 aboard.* This was going to be a bitch. He could just tell.

Chapter 9

Woods Hole

1700 hrs

Mac hung up from Blackie. The call had gone as expected. Black was his usual obnoxious self but had seemed to come around to some degree. The mission would be unpleasant anyway, and dealing with an ass would make it even more taxing, but at least he knew everything that could be done would happen.

Now all he needed was a ship, a crew, equipment, techs, and riggers. Hopefully he could select a group that wouldn't commit mutiny or kill Blackie and throw him over the side.

He walked back to the break room to get coffee.

Maddie stuck her head in the door. "Can I help? By the way, according to CNN, they're beginning to find floating debris."

"Interesting. Yes, I suppose you can. Start getting emails out to the sonar and photo techs and see who's available. Also, I'm sure others will be working on it as well, but see if we can get the information to *our* people so they can be doing wind drift and current analysis. I'll work on a ship, hardware, and riggers."

Maddie grinned and blushed slightly. "I'll be on it, Mac."

"I'm quite sure you will." He took his mug and headed back to his office and his whiteboards. Maybe someday he would be dragged into the computer generation. In the meantime, he began to set up his methods that had served him so well in the Navy. Charts, markers, maps. Primitive today, but Mac was a visual type of guy. That reminded him, he would need a good chart of the waters in the region with ocean depths. He'd have to tell Maddie. It didn't seem to matter what he wanted; she would find it, quickly.

First thing was a vessel. The yard superintendent, Thomas Sikes, would be the one who could tell him what the first available vessel would be. Mac needed a North-Atlantic-capable ship that hadn't actually started fall maintenance. Mac knew the ship he wanted, *Atlantis*. Picking up his phone, he called Sikes. "Hello, Thomas, how's your day going?"

"Same shit, different day, Mac. Can I assume this isn't a social call?"

"You know me too well. How soon could *Atlantis* be ready to go? It's an emergency."

"Yeah, I wondered about that when I saw the news. Actually I started looking at that this morning. With overtime authorization, she could be ready immediately. If you give me the go-ahead, we could be doing what little work *has* to be done while the riggers and techs are loading their gear. You could be underway within twenty four hours."

"Great news. Consider yourself authorized, from the Director through me."

"One problem, Mac. Jamison can't make it. His mother had a serious stroke a matter of hours ago. Unless he just up and left her, you don't have a skipper."

Mac thought for a moment. "Yes we do. Once I get the riggers and some techs working on loadout, I'll be onboard. Carry on. Get her ready. Maximum duration loadout. Work out where we can re-fuel somewhere near Greenland and get me a crew. Pull from any other ships to fill any holes. I know the timing sucks."

"Copy that. Oh, Mac, are you taking Blackie?"

"God help me, yeah, I am."

"It'll be okay, I think. Once he understands how important this is, he'll be on his best behavior. I'll put some Stoli on the provision list."

"May as well, no point in having to deal with that asshole sober."

"My thinking as well. I'll get on it. We'll have her ready, overtime be damned."

"Thanks, Thomas. I appreciate you."

"No problem, and if you need an engineer..."

"I'll call. Thanks again." Mac hung up the phone. The ship was arranged. Now for the technicians and the hardware. The North Atlantic in the fall was a cruel mistress. The sonar and photographic equipment they would need, along with the cables and data cables, needed to be duplicated.

Anything that could fail probably would in the hostile environment the Atlantic posed. The techs were good at repairs at sea, but it would be best to have a backup probe to keep the search underway rather than waiting for the primary device to be fixed. Sikes would handle loading the conex containers to house the terminal ends of the data. That was where the techs would sit watching the incredibly boring readouts from the towed sonars.

Oceanographic ships like the *Atlantis* were like seagoing semi-trucks. They were designed to carry crews and technicians to a location to hunt or investigate. The aft half of the vessels was open and multi-purpose. They carried winches at the stern, but forward from there, they could be configured for many different missions by simply loading containers with the needed electronic or biological labs for whatever the mission required.

Maddie walked in his door, startling him. "Sorry, boss, Blackie's on line three."

"Thanks." He took a deep breath and counted to ten. No telling how the conversation would go. "Hello, John. Any news for me?"

"Yeah, I'll be in on the train at about 2300 hrs. I suppose you can have someone there? Or should I get a cab?"

"No, I'll send someone. A cab would be a fortune."

"Okay. Oh, and, Mac, I read a paper. You're right. This is important. I'll be a good boy. By the way, is the Navy involved? I mean a U.S. flag airliner and all…"

"The director tells me he's working that angle. I recommended that he asked if the Navy could check the SOSUS hydrophones or divert a sub to the area to listen for the pingers in the flight data recorders and cockpit voice recorders. My guess is they want us to locate it, and then they'll get a salvage ship headed our way. But as I said, that's a guess. I think the whole situation is developing."

"Got it. Well, the train just pulled in. I'll call you if anything changes."

"Okay, and, John, thank you. We appreciate it. You and I both know you're the right man for the job."

"Copy that, see you later."

Mac hung up his phone. Was it possible? John Black would be a good boy? Nah, besides, he had decided not to tell Black that they would be on the same crew.

Chapter 10

September 10, 2003, 1530 hrs

Onboard Atlantis

Mac stood on the bridge wing of *Atlantis* looking back toward the stern. It was a sunny and pleasant early fall afternoon. The latest weather forecast for their search area had been fairly good that morning when he checked it. He watched as the large containers holding the sonar and video equipment labs were being secured and wired. There were hundreds of wires and cables to be connected from the remote probes. Power from the ship had to be connected to serve the lighting, computers, and heating and cooling.

Each box was the size that one might see stacked on a container ship or headed down the highways on a semi. Each was a totally self-contained lab, complete with work areas and seating for the techs that would operate and interpret information from the remote sensors that would be deployed deep below the surface of the North Atlantic.

Crews and equipment moved up and down the gangplank. Food and personnel comfort items were being loaded while the engineers toiled below decks taking care of last-minute details in the power plants, generators, and myriad other systems that would sustain Mac and his crew for about two weeks. After that, *Atlantis* would have to head for a port somewhere near the search area to re-fuel and re-provision, unless they got lucky early.

"Mac, your head sonar tech is on the bridge and wants to speak with you."

"Okay, be right in. Who'd we wind up with?" He knew most of the normal techs were gone. A few had hung around working in the labs, but most had split for who knew where when the oceaneering group had been placed on inactive status.

"King. C.A. King."

The name didn't ring a bell, which was odd. He thought he knew them all. Mac turned and walked the ten or so feet to the bridge door. He stepped over the half-foot sill that kept water out of the bridge in rough weather and walked inside, leaving to door open behind him.

"Good afternoon, Captain MacAdams. C.A. King reporting in. I wanted to introduce myself. It appears I'm your lead sonar tech."

Mac felt a strong handshake. He tried to disguise his surprise. C.A. King was a woman. She looked to be about thirty, five-two, slim, with glasses and her hair piled up under a Woods Hole ball cap. He looked her up and down quickly. She was dressed in jeans, work boots, and a Woods Hole windbreaker. Mac broke the handshake. "Er, yes. Of course. Welcome aboard, King, nice to meet you. Let's go back to the lounge and get some coffee. Follow me please."

Mac led her down a corridor from the bridge. His cabin was on the left, the lounge on the right. In the Navy, the room might have been known as the wardroom or officers' mess. Since *Atlantis* was a civilian vessel, there were no officers, per se, but out of courtesy the room was generally occupied only by members of the senior tech staff and department heads.

The room had two windows, a table with upholstered benches, and two couches. All bolted to the floor. One wall held a large and two smaller video display units, a computer terminal, and a player for training videos or to simply watch a movie after the evening meal. The opposite wall held a marine coffee maker, one where the coffee urns were firmly held in place, a microwave, and a newly installed expresso machine. A small refrigerator and supply shelving took up the space under the counter.

"Coffee?" Mac asked as he poured himself a mug.

"Sure, black please," King replied.

"Have a seat." Mac motioned her to one of the benches as he sat down across from her. "So, tell me about yourself, Miss King."

"Well, I joined Woods Hole a few weeks ago. Before that, I spent three years as a civilian employee with DOD specializing in design and operation of side-scan sonar. I worked on sonar for minesweepers, subs, and sub hunters. Prior to that, I worked for six years in the private sector after college building sonars and writing technical manuals for them."

"Where did you attend college?"

"MIT."

"I didn't attend college."

"Yes, I had heard that, Mr. MacAdams. The word is that you're the epitome of old school."

Mac smiled. "I suppose that's pretty accurate. But someone doesn't drop in my opinion if they went to college. By the way, I'm sure that my surprise showed, but I want to make sure you understand that I have no problems with a woman performing any job on this mission. As long as she's competent."

"Glad to hear it."

"On the other hand, you'll be working for Black, and I'm not sure he shares the same opinion."

"Would that be John Fucking Black?"

"Indeed it would." Mac smiled. "It would seem you're aware of Mr. Black's history."

"Let's just say I've heard about him. Word around the lab is that Mr. Black considers himself something of a ladies' man and that he doesn't appreciate being shot down."

"That's probably accurate, Miss King."

"Please, we're going to be together for a while, sir. I'd prefer you either call me Cat or King. My birth certificate says Carol Anne King. Since high school I've usually been known as Cat, or 'hey nerd.' So...call me Cat?"

"Done. As I was saying, however, John Black is a very unusual and talented individual. He has some demons, he can be lower than pond scum, his manners are atrocious, but damn it, he gets the job done when no one else can."

Mac leaned back against the cushion, studying Cat's reaction. She *did* have a bit of a nerdish look about her. Her glasses weren't stylish. She seemed to be wearing little or no makeup. There was a faint sign of Asian influence in her bloodline. She seemed to have the look of the librarian that was ultra conservative, until she let her hair down and lost the glasses.

She also seemed just a few years older than Mac's granddaughter, so regardless of how hot she actually might be, he couldn't see anything but a professional relationship developing with King.

"So, may I call you Mac?"

"Of course, Cat, Mac is fine."

"Okay then. I'll be on deck checking out the sonar. If you need me, I'm available, any time."

"Thank you. I look forward to working with you." Mac stood and shook hands with her. She turned and left the wardroom. Mac followed her out and walked across the hall to his cabin. Closing the door behind him, he picked up the shore phone and called Maddie's extension.

"Yes, Mac, how can I help?"

"I need you to find out everything you can about a C.A. King. She's working for Woods Hole, and she's going to be on *Atlantis* as lead sonar tech. I need her personnel file and anything that's not in her personnel file as soon as possible."

"Gotcha, boss. Are you looking for anything in particular?"

"No..."

"You've just got a feeling, right?"

"Exactly. Something just seems a bit too perfect."

"Okay, I'm on it. I'll send it over by courier or carry it myself as soon as I have something."

"Thanks, Maddie, you're the best."

"I know. Get back to work, boss."

He hung up. In very little time, Maddie would have a dossier on C.A. King that a would tell Mac whatever he needed to know.

Chapter 11

Mac was having dinner in the wardroom with his department heads. It was a final check, going around the horn in preparation for departure. They dined on takeout tonight, Pizza Hut to be precise. The engineer indicated the ship was ready, fueled, fresh water tanks full, and, in general, ready to pull out.

On the other hand, the cook was cursing about a few missing items and a baking oven that needed a minor repair. The techs were just a few hours from being complete with work that needed to be done with access to shore facilities. Cat reported sonar was ready to perform a final all-up dry test. Calibration would still have to be performed, but that would be done on station.

"Where's Blackie?" Mac asked. The people at the table looked at each other then back at Mac with a collective "We have no clue" look on their faces.

Oddly enough, Black chose that time to enter the room. "Hi, everyone, I'm sorry I'm late. I've just completed downloading some location information for our target. Through some sources that shall, of course, have to remain nameless, we have information provided by the DOD."

"How do you feel about it, John?" queried Mac.

"I have info from SOSUS, as well as pings picked up by an attack sub transiting the general area. My suggestion is we use these in conjunction with what Woods Hole oceanographers have worked out based on backtracking floating debris. To be perfectly honest, none of the information agrees. My suggestion is we plot all three and throw a dart at a point in the center."

"Okay, John, we have to start somewhere. We'll use your dart as an initial epicenter and begin mowing the lawn. Okay, everyone, based on what information I have, my mind is made up. We'll leave the pier at 0000 hrs, so everyone inform your people. Any objections?" He looked around the room. "Okay then, you have a little less than five hours. Get busy or take a nap, I don't care. Either way, the bus is leaving." Mac smiled.

Someone had to make the call, and he was happy to do so, politely of course.

The room emptied as people finished their pizza. John sat down and grabbed a plate, loading three pieces of pepperoni on it. "So, Mac, how do you feel about the mission?"

"Well, I'd love something a little more definite, but it's less than we had when Ballard found *Titanic*. By the way, what's the radius of your three points?"

"It's not as bad as it could be. From the center, the most different point is about ten thousand meters out. Could be worse. Oh, by the way, as I was leaving the offices, Maddie gave me this to hand deliver to you." He handed over a manila envelope. "She said it was urgent."

Mac surmised it was the report on King. "Thanks. Is your gear aboard?"

"Affirmative. I'm rooming with the engineer. My go bag is in a locker that I have the only key to. I'll get it copied right away and give you one."

"I'm guessing your go bag has things in it that would never make it through carry-on."

"You know me well, and let's both hope I don't need any of it. By the way, I assume the no-smoking ban is waived at sea?"

"Hmm, there have been some recent changes. Smoke all you like on deck, otherwise forget it. You aren't *that* special. Do we understand each other?"

"Yeah, I get it. It'll be fine. I won't bitch." Black looked at MacAdams and almost grinned. "Seriously, I won't raise a fuss, you'll see." He turned and walked away.

Mac waited for Blackie to leave and then rolled his eyes. Blackie not raising a fuss? Seriously? And something felt very, very wrong about his lead sonar tech. This mission reeked to high heaven, and they hadn't even left the dock.

He turned his attention to the manila envelope. Maddie would have answers. There were roughly ten pages of computer printouts in the envelope, along with a handwritten page. That was significant in and of itself. Maddie only handwrote two things; Post-it notes or shit she didn't want anyone else to see other than the recipient of the note. This was unquestionably the latter.

He unfolded the sheet.

Mac – You were correct. There's definitely something wrong with C.A. King's history. First, what's actually there is way too perfect. Perfect enough I would bet anything it's manufactured. I followed her back to the womb, basically. She's not assumed an alternate identity. Her history looks totally normal until MIT. There were three semesters at MIT, during which she disappeared. No comments entered in her transcript. This is standard operating procedure for someone being groomed by the Agency. Then, during her DOD and private sector career, there are unexplained gaps. They exceed what would be allowed by anyone as sick or on vacation leave, but there are no negative comments.

Also, there's her passport. Passports are good for ten years, as you know. Hers has been re-issued four times in nine years. That would only happen if you didn't want people to know where you've been, and with cooperation from the State Department.

Mac, bottom line. There's nothing that says she's evil, but she's a spook. I'd bet you a signed Clive Cussler hardback on it - M.

There it was, proof positive. Cat was a spook. Mac had known there was something "wrong." CIA wasn't his first inclination, hell, there was nothing that actually said that was a bad thing for that matter, but why did the Agency want a spook at Woods Hole? And, most importantly, how would he deal with it and at what point did he confront Cat with the fact that he was on to her? When it was time, obviously.

Chapter 12

September 14, 2003 0900 hrs

Onboard Atlantis

Southeast of Greenland

Mac sat in his chair on the bridge. *Atlantis* was "mowing the lawn" under partly cloudy skies with a wind and seas blowing gently out of the northwest. A search area established, the next stage was to subdivide the area into quadrants and begin towing the side-scan sonar back and forth with a fifty percent overlap on a thousand-meter cable about three hundred meters off the ocean floor.

The sonar sensor resembled a torpedo. The yellow, two-meter-long metal tube had a wad of wiring in its innards, four tail fins at its rear, and an attachment point with multiple cables tethering it to the ship at the surface. The sensor sent a directional beam of sound out and listened with sensors that transmitted a real-time "picture" to the displays on *Atlantis*. The side-scan sonar gave a realistic, near-photo-quality image of whatever lay under it as *Atlantis* towed it across the bottom.

"Hits" would be logged by GPS for further exploration with a towed camera, but the first priority would be mapping the bottom and identifying and cataloging targets for a closer look.

The sonar crew, Cat included, was sequestered in their trailer, doing the incredibly boring job of watching the readout on several monitors. Since John was technically the principle investigator, he and Cat met daily. Mac's observation of their interaction indicated that John trusted Cat and left her alone unless she came to him for his opinion. Subsurface investigation resembled combat, hours upon hours of incredible boredom interspersed with moments of unbelievable excitement. The difference was that, in combat, the excitement was usually accompanied by panic and adrenaline-pumping fear, and sometimes by death.

Mac sat in the captain's chair on the bridge, but in truth, he was nothing but a passenger right now. The autopilot was guiding *Atlantis*, with the helmsman, Jeff, simply watching the GPS tick off distance until the next turn point. Mac flipped a page in his Cussler novel. Might as well get some reading in while *Atlantis* plowed through the six-foot seas at a whopping three knots. The speed was determined by several factors. The sonar techs had a maximum limit impacting their readouts. The riggers had another maximum set by the amount of strain on the tow cable and umbilical transmitting data back to the ship. As long as the ship didn't exceed either maximum, all was well.

"Mac, got a moment?"

He turned to see Blackie standing at his side.

"Sure, what's up?" Mac placed the book jacket in his book to hold his place and swiveled his chair to face John.

"What do you know about our sonar tech?"

He knows something too! This was going to be a problem; he could sense it. "I think I know enough, why?"

John looked at him with a poorly disguised grin. "If you know, no problem. I just wanted to bring her past to your attention."

"Let's just say I don't know everything, but I know she isn't simply a sonar tech with a degree from MIT and an extensive background in the field. Is there something we should discuss in private?"

"No, not yet."

"Do you see any problems with her work?"

"No, on the contrary, she seems to have her shit together. She understands the hardware; she has a good handle of our software. It's just…"

"Just what?"

Blackie shrugged. "I don't know. I just wanted to bounce it off you."

"Duly noted, John. On another topic, did you note we laid in a supply of Stoli?"

John broke into a grin. "That I did. Appreciate it." He gave Mac a gentle punch in the shoulder and turned to walk away. "Again, I won't abuse your consideration. My intention is to be on my best behavior."

"For what it's worth, you've been incredibly well behaved. How are we doing from a principle investigator standpoint?"

"Well, in all honesty, everything is going quite well. We've acquired three or four potential points worthy of investigation, so given the percentage of the target area we've covered, that's about what I'd expect. It's early yet. You understand how it works. The equipment and the people are doing what they need to do."

"Will you try to see me a couple times a day to just give me an informal brief?"

John smiled. "Of course. That's a reasonable request, be glad to." He turned and left the bridge, cigarette and lighter in hand.

Mac settled back into his chair and pulled his Cussler novel back into his lap. He knew there was, in all likelihood, something seriously wrong with Blackie being this cooperative, but since he had no clue why John was being so well behaved, he decided worrying about it was pointless. He had learned long ago there was nothing to be gained by worrying about shit that was totally outside his control. In this case those things consisted of weather, reliability of hardware, and John Fucking Black.

He reached forward to the counter below the bridge windows and grabbed his walkie-talkie. "Cat, this is Mac."

"Copy you, Mac, how may I be of assistance?"

"Cat, when you have time, can you send me a paper plot of potential targets located so far?"

There was a brief pause. "Yes, sir, I'll have someone run it up to you within five or ten minutes."

"Copy that. Thank you," he replied. Mac believed in saying thank you. Two simple words. He knew it was understood that his request was, in essence, an order, but the simple addition of a thank you had always seemed to him to be an inexpensive addition of simple manners. The military didn't require it, but even then, he had used those two words unless time was of the essence.

He knew Cat had likely rolled her eyes. The information he requested was available on the computer monitor showing search results. Plotting the information to paper would require a few minutes, which would seem totally unnecessary to someone like Cat, but dammit, Mac liked paper.

A few Cussler pages later, a young sonar minion with dark hair and a track suit arrived with a small stack of computer paper in hand. "Excuse me, sir," he spoke, handing over the printouts, "Ms. King sent me up with these for you."

He held the papers out for Mac. The young man seemed a little old for a grad student, and English didn't sound like his first language. "Thanks, and you are...?"

"Hameed, sir, I'm a transfer from Oxford. Ms. King asked me along to help fill in a hole in the shifts. I'm proud to be associated with this team and Woods Hole in general." The young man bowed, almost an overly excessive bow.

"Thank you, Hameed, I hope we meet again. Welcome board."

"Thank you, sir, will there be anything else?"

"No, thank you, not right now."

Hameed turned quickly and left. Mac made a mental note to email Maddie. He felt an urge to learn more about Hameed.

Chapter 13

September 16, 2003
 0200 hrs
Onboard Atlantis
Southeast of Greenland

A halfway gentle knock on his door awakened Mac. He glanced around his roughly eighty-square-foot cabin briefly to see why he was awake when the knock was repeated. "Come," he mumbled, sitting up. Blackie strode in, seeming wide awake and excited.

"Can you come down to the sonar lab, Mac? We've got a target I want you to look at. I think we should break the search pattern and set up to send a photo ROV down."

"Looks that promising?"

"Definitely, but that's my opinion. You're the boss."

"What are you getting on the side-scan?"

"You need to see it yourself."

"Be down in ten minutes. What's the coffee situation?"

"I'll get some real coffee ready by the time you get there. You know how these youngsters are. They either want expresso or some crazy tea shit. We need a Starbucks onboard. We could make a friggin' fortune."

Mac smiled. He and Blackie were on the same page when it came to coffee; they both liked Navy coffee. One step away from battery acid, the staler the better. God help anyone that actually washed a coffee pot Mac drank from. Any individual that disturbed the fine patina on the innards of an ex-navy man's coffee pot would risk correction in a most severe manner.

He pulled on a pair of jeans and a sweatshirt and then slipped into his deck shoes. As he left his cabin, he made a point to walk through the bridge, smiling and greeting the night crew. Mac made an effort to visit each phase of the small ship's operation at different hours of the day and night, always trying to greet the crewmembers with a smile and some form of encouragement. The cost was minimal, and the benefits were large in his opinion.

"Hi, guys, everything good?"

His answer was a generic nod from each of the two men occupying the bridge at two a.m.

"I'm headed down to sonar. We may be turning back on a target. Don't do it yet, but we may need to wake up some riggers to haul in the towed sonar and deploy an ROV. Just a head's-up."

"Copy that, sir, we'll be ready to wake 'em up." One young man grinned, seeming happy to interrupt someone's rest.

Mac made his way toward the stern. The early fall weather was cool. The seas were unusually calm, and *Atlantis* had only a slight pitch and roll as she made her way through the cold seas southeast of Greenland. He smelled the diesel exhaust as he made his way to the trailer. He found John Black just outside the door, cigarette in hand.

"Morning, John, getting a last one in before we go inside?" Mac grinned a little as the two shook hands.

"You know me too well. Coffee's on, should be ready by now. Let's go." Black turned away from Mac and opened the door. The two stepped into the lair of the geeks. The trailer was crammed with electronic gizmos everywhere, and it was dimly lit, deliberately. A rack of servers split the trailer. On the left side, counters for a few conveniences. A microwave, a mini-refrigerator, coffee pot, and assorted bags of chips and questionable portions of sandwiches and food and drinks littered the counter to the point that there was no room to place anything much larger than a Coke can anywhere.

The heart of the trailer was on the right side of the servers. There were three comfortable chairs on rollers, a twenty-foot-long counter, and countless video display units. This was presently Ms. King's empire, and she sat in the center chair before the screens. She noticed Mac and John approaching, mugs of coffee in hand.

She turned in her chair and smiled. "Good morning, nice to see you in my world." King seemed to have been there for some time. She definitely didn't appear to have been roused from a sound sleep like Mac.

When he thought about it, his lead sonar tech seemed to take her job very seriously. Mac's informal observations of her work hours placed her in this trailer roughly twenty hours a day. She seemed to break for naps and an occasional meal or shower. Amazingly, though, she seemed to be upbeat and, like the Energizer Bunny, constantly in motion. Perhaps she had a fear that stopping might result in her falling asleep for three days.

"Morning. Blackie says you have something to show me, and since he woke me up, it must be significant."

"He's right. Hameed, let Mac have your seat and bring up the recording."

The young man stood, and Mac slid into his chair. Mac watched as Hameed typed commands into one of the many computer keyboards on the counter. Mac knew everything that came from the sonar probe was recorded in a hard drive and a tape backup as well.

Mac watched as the side-scan sonar readout came up on the monitor. The display had a lot of information, but it was easy to decipher. In the upper left hand corner, a digital readout showed the date and time in GMT, or Greenwich Mean Time. Glancing at his Rolex GMT Master, he could see this display was a little over an hour old.

Under that was a readout of the GPS location for the ship, in this case *Atlantis*. In the upper right hand corner, a readout showed the GPS location and depth of the probe. Obviously a probe several thousand meters below the surface couldn't "see" the GPS satellites, but Mac knew, when the probe was launched from the stern of the ship, the current GPS coordinates were entered into the probe's navigation system. From that point on, an inertial navigation system in the probe calculated this information.

Depth below the surface and off the bottom were also displayed. Empty water was displayed in black, the bottom in green, and any anomalies, or objects, were displayed in red or yellow, depending on the "hardness" of the echo return. Currently a green, slightly undulating bottom cruised from right to left on the monitor. Occasional yellow blobs tracked by. Pointing at one, he turned to Cat. "What are these?"

"Rocks," she replied, smiling. "Some of them are as big as *Atlantis*. The glaciers pushed them off Greenland hundreds of thousands of years ago."

"Interesting…" he mumbled, *but hardly worth waking my ass up.* Just before he shared his thoughts with Ms. King and her minions, a very familiar-looking red-colored triangle moved slowly across the screen. "That's an aircraft tail!"

"Exactly, and it's the reason you're down here instead of in your comfortable rack," Blackie proudly proclaimed. "As I said, I'd like to break with mowing the lawn and set up a much smaller grid search to define the debris field."

Mac stood. He looked at Cat and shook her hand. "Nice work. If you and John will put your heads together, I've given the bridge instructions to be prepared to change the search pattern."

"Thank you, sir. Stuff like this is about the only break we get from boredom."

Mac turned and left the console. Black walked ahead of him.

As they exited the trailer, John stopped, turning to Mac. "Got a sec?"

John stopped. "Sure."

Black fiddled in his jacket pocket and fished out two shot glasses. He grinned, handed one to Mac, and went to another pocket to pull out a stainless flask. "Share a celebration shot with me?"

"Why not?" Mac answered. "Stoli?"

"Only the best, Captain," he replied as he poured the glasses quite full.

As the two drank their vodka silently, Mac's mind went back in time, remembering the good, and the bad, times he and John Black had spent together. He also recalled why John had a middle name that only those who knew him well would use. No doubt John was recalling similar incidents in his history with Mac. The two had never really fought. They had an enormous clash of personalities, of means and methods. But as the vodka warmed Mac's throat, he thought this trip was showing genuine glimmers of change in John.

Black finished his Stoli and put the shot glass back in his pocket, digging out a pack of smokes as he did. "One more out here on deck, and then I'll go back inside and scope out a plan with Cat. Thanks for having a drink with me. Brought back old times."

"That it did, my old friend." Mac handed John his empty shot glass and slapped John on the shoulder. He turned and headed for the bridge.

Chapter 14

September 16, 2003

2200 hrs

Onboard Atlantis

Southeast of Greenland

Atlantis was currently stationary over the debris field located some twenty hours earlier. Holding station in the North Atlantic was no easy feat. Had it not been for GPS technology and the fact that *Atlantis* had bow and stern thrusters to keep the ship within roughly fifty meters of a desired position, it would have been nearly impossible in the present conditions.

Seas had picked up to roughly eight-foot-wave heights, and the winds were blowing a nearly constant twenty kilometers per hour. Holding station on a set point meant half the crew was either sick or taking enough drugs to stop puking but be in a semi-awake mode due to the side effects of the anti-nausea drugs.

Then again, some members of the crew seemed to be immune to the constant tossing and rolling of the ship. Mac and Blackie were in that group.

At present it was quite dark on the surface. A remote-operated vehicle, or ROV, was presently on its way down to the debris field. This particular robot was a Woods-Hole-developed unit called a Nereus by the company. On *Atlantis*, and in the second conex at the stern, the robot's name was Homer, as in Homer Simpson.

Homer was about the size of a refrigerator. He was yellow and equipped in this particular mission with extra lights, still cameras, and a closed-circuit video camera to send real time video back to his operators in the conex. Homer could also be equipped with an arm and a grappling device, but Cat and Blackie had made the decision to forego the grapple on this mission.

The ROV headed into the deep in a static mode, saving power. That meant the four propellers mounted in the unit were resting, waiting for input from its pilot. Once Homer reached the bottom, two people would take over. Karen, a twenty-something brunette nerd and a new member of the ROV team would operate the cameras while a young, crewcut member who went by the name of Evan would "fly" Homer under the direction of Cat and Blackie.

Cat had left the conex and gone outside. There were several reasons, all bad at this point. She had taken an opportunity to puke over the side first, second to sneak a smoke, and, last, to look for John effing Black. He was late again. King assumed he was either smoking, drinking, or both in some hiding spot she had not yet discovered. In this case, however, she was incorrect. John was in Mac's cabin behind a locked door.

"So you're quite convinced this plane isn't the 747?"

"I'm sure of it. We have to put eyes on it to confirm I'm right, but I can prove it in just a few minutes based on the sonar imaging." He handed over a two-by-three-foot plot of the debris field. There were eight circles drawn on the plot with a felt tip. Each was numbered and had a description under it. "First let me, state the obvious. The entire debris field only has a seven-hundred-meter radius."

"That's impossible!"

"Well, impossible for an aircraft blown up at thirty-five thousand feet. But you're right. When we find the *right* jet, there will be miles separating the lighter material ejected from the fuselage at the time the bomb detonated from the heavy stuff like engines."

"I'm in absolute agreement. Plus, based on this scan, the fuselage appears more or less intact on this wreckage."

"You're observant. In fact, let's look at the obvious on the fuselage itself. Based on the scans, it's too short and too narrow. There's no way this is Flight 92. Here, one more deciding point. You mentioned engines. Here's a blow-up of a scan of an engine apparently torn off during the crash."

Mac looked at it for a few moments, turning it upside down and back. "That's it, proof positive. This is a double-engine nacelle, and unless I miss my guess, it came off something belonging to the Air Force. Maybe a BUFF."

John's tone of voice changed, as did his demeanor. He leaned forward and was nearly whispering when he replied, "That's exactly what it is. There's more. Due to some insanely unlikely chain of events, I'm one of three or four people on the planet that know the full story of this particular aircraft and the potential disaster lurking on the bottom of the ocean right below us."

Mac pondered what he had heard, processing both the words and the implications. "Okay. I'm not sure I want to know any more about this wreckage, John. So, correct me if I'm wrong, but I would think we need to be sitting in the conex when Homer reaches the bottom, state the obvious that this isn't Flight 92, and instruct everyone to get Homer back onboard and resume our grid search. Agreed?"

John nodded and stood. "Yes, that's exactly what we need to do. You've always been able to cut to the chase, and in a hurry. Just do your best to act disappointed about Flight 92 and uninterested in the wreck we're parked on right now. That would be my recommendation."

Mac stood, prompting John to do the same. The two shook hands, and Blackie took his leave, quietly closing Mac's cabin door behind him. Mac had reached for his jacket in preparation to head to the conex when he heard his walkie-talkie beep.

"Mac, Cat here. Could you please come to the conex? Homer is almost to the bottom, and have you seen John?"

He keyed the radio and replied, "I'll be headed that way in a moment, Miss King, and no, I haven't seen John."

"He should've been here by now. Shit. I suppose he's hiding somewhere drinking again. Okay, see you in a few, out."

Mac clicked his push-to-talk button twice to signify he had heard her and they were done for now. In a sense, it was mildly funny. Cat was mad at John for being a drunk, which was, for the most part, quite true. She also assumed he was absent because of his affinity for alcohol and nicotine, which, in this case, was patently false.

Mac wasn't quite able to feel sympathy for Blackie; his reputation preceded him for a reason. In this particular case, however, Cat's suspicions were wrong, and Mac hoped she realized it when they all arrived at the conex to see what Homer had to show them.

2300 hrs
Inside the ROV conex

Mac had been wrong. Then again, maybe he wasn't. He had entered the van to find everyone on site. Cat and her staff seated at their stations before the wall of monitors. Homer's pilot looked as if he was in a video gamer's heaven. There were two joysticks before him, directing Homer's movements. He had one small video display from the robot's camera and two more displays showing him Homer's place on the bottom in both the horizontal and vertical axis.

Mac was disappointed because, for reasons of his own, Blackie had arrived at the conex a mere fifteen minutes after he had left Mac's cabin. In that time, he had managed to be acting, and smelling, like he had just left a bar. Mac secretly suspected Black was sober as a judge, right now anyway. So why did he want Cat to think he was drunk? There was something going on, and Mac intended to get to the bottom of it. But not tonight.

Homer's pilot, Evan, reported, "We're on station on the bottom. I'm not entirely sure exactly where we are, so we'll run to the north until we see a target we've established in the debris field. That should tell us exactly where we are."

Cat, who was acting as the team leader at this point, replied, "Agreed, Evan. North it is."

Everyone in the conex watched the live CCTV image as Homer moved approximately ten meters off the ocean floor.

Evan, Cat, and Karen were seated at the three seats at the counter, monitors galore in front of them. Mac, Blackie, and a few others stood behind them, gazing at the color monitors displaying the live feed from Homer's camera.

Homer was fighting about a three-knot current on the ocean floor. With a top speed of six knots, it meant the robot moved at about a three-knot speed. Even though the debris field was relatively small, at the present rate, it would take quite a while to cover a significant part of the target area.

Thankfully, Homer was also equipped with a short-range sonar unit with a display of its own. Karen was monitoring the sonar intently, prepared to give Evan direction to find objects worth obtaining video.

"Okay, Evan, I've got a hard target about one hundred meters, twenty degrees right," Karen directed calmly.

"Copy, twenty right," Evan replied.

Mac watched the monitors pan by as a sandy ocean bottom passed before the group gathered around the team. He kept Blackie's comments relating the fact that they were on a wreck site unrelated to the objective to himself as they neared a target.

"Twenty meters, "Karen stated.

Evan didn't reply.

Visibility on the bottom was only about ten meters. The currents swept sand and silt toward the cameras on Homer as the robot traveled along the ocean floor.

"I've got something coming up," Evan informed the group.

As they watched, an object came into view. It looked like a piece of wing laying on the bottom. As Homer came closer, it became apparent they were seeing a wing tip and about ten meters of wing attached. Evan made a slight right turn to move down the wing laterally.

They all watched intently as the camera revealed more of the wing.

"Okay, I'm thinking this is target seven on the debris field," Cat narrated calmly.

At that point a double engine nacelle came into view, verifying this particular piece of wing was upside down.

"I hate to say it, but it looks like this isn't Flight 92." Mac voiced an opinion. "No way this is a 747."

"Shit!" Cat exclaimed in a relatively quiet manner. "I agree, Mac. You're right. What do we do? I mean we're already here."

"I understand. Let's do this. Based on your plot, give Evan a vector for the fuselage. We'll see if we can get a tail number so we can pass it along to the probable owner, and then we pack it in and get back on a grid search." He glanced toward John, looking for feedback. Hell, he had to tell them something.

Blackie looked at him and shrugged and gave a slight nod.

Mac read it as a qualified approval.

"Very well, I concur. Evan, 210 degrees should head you toward the fuselage."

"Copy that, 210 degrees it is," Evan acknowledged.

Mac watched as Homer proceeded across the ocean floor. He knew what the outcome *should* be, and knew John did as well, but accepted the fact that he had to act like no one else was aware of what the probable outcome would be.

The team stared at the monitors as Homer traversed the predominantly sandy ocean floor as it headed toward what the sonar had indicated was the fuselage.

At the speed the robot was moving, the trek toward the next known target seemed to take forever, but it was actually only five or ten minutes.

Karen casually announced, "Homer's sonar says there's a target coming up." She could say that because the short-range sonar in Homer could "see" roughly one hundred meters ahead, whereas the cameras could only show what the combination of lights and optics revealed. That was limited to about ten meters at best.

"Okay, what I see on the radar tells me this is the tail section. It shows the vertical stabilizer, looks like there's some mangling. Should be coming in sight right...about...now!"

Indeed, it did. The group in the conex watched several monitors as gray metal began to come into view. Homer was transmitting a continuous stream back to *Atlantis*. The stream went to multiple recorders. As they watched, they could see occasional flashes as

Karen triggered still photos accompanied by strobes that fired.

They watched as the mangled horizontal stabilizers came into the small halo of light emitted by the robot. Interested sea life casually drifted up to examine the uninvited visitor to their neighborhood. Others scurried away. At three-thousand meters below the surface, life forms were scarce, and odd.

"Hold there please," Cat ordered quietly. "Ease up a bit and do a slow pan until we can get a look at any markings on the tail. Do everything in slow motion. We can't be kicking up silt with the props."

Evan nodded. "You got it." He did exactly as asked, and the little yellow robot responded as Evan eased the joystick controllers in slow motion. His hands moved like a cross between a skilled gamer and a surgeon.

Mac found it very satisfying to watch the interplay between the members of the team. Maybe he hadn't actually trained any of them, but he had assembled the team and transported them to this place.

"Hold right there please," Cat ordered. Everyone in the van peered at the image of the forty-odd-foot-tall tail. The aluminum structure showed minor signs of corrosion, but not that much. At temperatures slightly above freezing, and with a very low oxygen content, the wreck was quite well preserved. The problem was that the metal showed signs of having been originally painted in a medium gray color with black letters and numbers on it.

While the base metal itself was remarkably well preserved, the paint, not so much. Karen was snapping photo after photo, the strobes popping every few seconds. If the paint weathering wasn't bad in and of itself, the entire tail seemed to be coated with a film that could have been silt or a bacterial film. Most likely it was a combination of the two.

What was obvious was that this was definitely not a civilian aircraft. At the base of the vertical stabilizer, actually at the extreme rear of the fuselage itself, two gun barrels extended out of the gray metal tube that formed the tail of the aircraft. Unless 747s were now equipped with small cannons, they were definitely looking at the wrong aircraft.

Cat tapped a pen on the counter before her, a habit she demonstrated when she was nervous or puzzled. "Okay, can anyone make out anything on the tail that would tell us exactly which bomber we're dealing with here?"

Silence. It seemed she was not alone.

"May I make a suggestion?" Evan spoke up.

"I'm all ears. What are you thinking?" King replied.

"If I hold Homer in his present position and go to max thrust in reverse, it might blow enough shit away so we can read something. I'll get moved out of visible range for a bit, but I can put us right back here without a lot of trouble."

"Do it," she replied with no hesitation.

To the spectators watching over the shoulders of the team, the result seemed dramatic and catastrophic. The scene before them totally disappeared in a cloud of grayish silt. Homer's lights illuminated the silt like headlights in the fog, and the effective viewing area was a cloud of swirling junk one or two meters in front of the lens and that was it.

"That blew us about five or six meters away from where we were. I'm shutting the lights down and telling Homer to hold in place. Give it two or three minutes and the currents should blow away the silt. We can go back in and look then," Evan announced calmly to everyone.

Mac stood with everyone else, waiting to see what was or wasn't visible on the tail. Personally, he hoped the tail gave no specifics. From what John Black had told him, there was something very disturbing about this aircraft. He had no idea if it had something to do with the cargo, the crew, or something else, but Mac hoped this wreckage was unidentifiable.

Unfortunately, overruling Cat's desire to get a tail number would have drawn suspicion that he hoped to avoid. His thoughts were interrupted by Evan.

"Okay, moving back in now."

Mac, and everyone else, watched as the large tail section came back into view, slowly coming into Homer's lights, yards and yards of metal appearing from the black, cold void. It had helped. The deterioration of the paint had left the numbers and letters impossible to read.

"I think I can solve this," Karen announced, snapping one still photo after another. "I can open these photos with software and process them. I'm pretty sure I can sort this out given a few hours."

Cat spoke. "Okay then, anybody see any need to linger?"

No one replied. "Very well then. Let's pack it in and get back to searching for a 747, ladies and gentlemen. Thanks." She stood and removed her headset and bolted for the door.

Mac knew she was headed for the rail to vomit because he could see it in her eyes as she passed him. As he walked out, Blackie caught up with him as he walked out onto the aft deck of *Atlantis*.

"Mac, was there anything on the tail you recognized?"

"Yes, the emblem."

"Exactly, my friend. It was very faint; the youngsters may not have recognized it. Perhaps you have some idea now of the nightmare we've stumbled upon."

Mac did, and it worried him to no end. While the letters and numbers on the bomber's tail were illegible, for now at least, the emblem had been unmistakable, at least to him. It was the crest of the Strategic Air Command, the part of the U.S. Air Force tasked with carrying, and potentially delivering, nuclear weapons.

Mac, Atlantis, and his team had located the plane, and now it seemed possible that there were atom bombs laying on the ocean floor two miles below his feet. That thought chilled him much more than the damp night air. It was a chill that his jacket would not keep out.

Chapter 15

Martin Parks, USAF(ret), walked into his den. He opened his wood stove and threw two more logs in the coals and stirred the ashes with a poker. The small cabin located in the Sangre de Cristo mountain range was at an elevation of nearly six thousand feet, and the September air was crisp in the morning.

The beautiful, small cabin bordered the Carson National Forest, and the views were simply majestic. Parks and his wife had the cabin constructed as a getaway from the huge home in Taos they had retired to after his career with the Air Force ended. It had always been their plan to move there one day to revel in nature with the hiking and skiing close by.

Their plans, or his plans at least, had changed when his wife of thirty-odd years had left for greener pastures in the form of a younger, well-connected, active-duty Air Force general.

For the second time in Parks' life, the military had robbed him of his potential, of his happiness. The first time was when Parks himself had committed career suicide by threatening to go over the head of General Lemay over the loss of Broadway Two Four and its cargo. Parks had eventually surrendered to Lemay, after Lemay had quietly threatened him with disgrace and potentially prison. Naturally, his career had stalled.

Parks was bitter, and in all honesty, he supposed that bitterness had possibly planted the seeds of his divorce. His wife had held on until he retired. Whether she had done so out of greed or frustration resulting from his inability to enjoy the retired life he and June had planned, he would never know.

All he knew was that her delay in serving him with papers until after his retirement resulted in her leaving with part of that retirement, as well as their home while she shacked up with her new beau. The kids were grown. They and the grandchildren had sided with June, saying Parks was a bastard no sane woman should be forced to live with and had abandoned him to the cabin in the mountains. To presumably die. Alone.

Parks made coffee and carried it to the portion of the den he had configured as his office and booted up his computer. He scanned through CNN to see if anything significant had changed in the world overnight. One story was interesting, it seemed Woods Hole was in the process of searching for the downed airliner. Nothing else seemed worth reading, so he opened his email program. Who knew, maybe some idiot wanted to meet a bastard to play golf or just get drunk again.

He felt a chill pass over him when he saw the name of one of the senders – JFB. John Fucking Black. He hadn't heard from Blackie for over fifteen years. Parks could hardly say they were friends. As with most, he found dealing with Black to be a less-than-enjoyable proposition. The two had only one thing in common, knowledge of a secret that no more than a handful of people shared.

Parks remembered their first meeting. Black had taken a seat at the bar in the clubhouse of the golf course on Warner Robbins Air Force Base in Georgia. After buying Parks a second Jack Daniels, and briefly bullshitting about the weather, he had told Parks he needed to have a private discussion with him on a matter of "great importance."

Parks had blown him off at the time, but not before Blackie handed him a business card. The card seemed odd. John Black – U.S. Navy. That and a telephone number with an 800 prefix. Period. His curiosity piqued, Parks looked into Black. He had, after all, not looked anything like anyone connected with the Navy, or any other branch of service for that matter. When he approached him, Black was wearing chinos, a golf shirt, and a blue blazer. That didn't seem especially odd. The beard, ponytail, and the gold Rolex submariner *did* seem totally out of place.

Parks had returned to his office. He was still a colonel, but instead of being in SAC, he commanded a maintenance squadron of cargo planes. It was one of a long series of shit jobs the Air Force had assigned him to after his run-in with Lemay. He was two years from having his thirty in and taking retirement. Parks picked up his phone and started to call his secretary in to have her look into Black and then thought better of it.

Instead, he went to a computer at the public library a day later and looked into John Black. What was available was puzzling indeed. Black had a Ph.D. in nuclear physics from MIT and had worked in the private sector before becoming a naval officer, assigned to a sub. From there, he had disappeared from commercially available databases.

Parks almost dialed the number on the card more than once but decided instead to avoid Black like the plague. With only two years left, Black could be toxic to his career. Black could be with military intelligence, oxymoron as it was, or something worse.

He found Black to be a persistent bastard, and informed as well, at least with regards to Parks' schedule. They met again at the club a week later.

"Good afternoon, Colonel," Black remarked, sliding into the bar stool next to Parks. "You haven't called me."

"You're very observant. That would because I have no need or desire to discuss anything with you. Great importance be damned, and don't bother to buy me a drink. I won't be here longer than it takes to finish this one."

Black never said a word. He ordered a drink for himself and sat silently beside Parks, smoking a cigarette. When he noticed Parks turning up his glass, he calmly reached for a cocktail napkin and pulled out a pen. He jotted something on the napkin, folded it, and slid it in front of Parks. Killing his drink in one gulp, he stubbed out his smoke.

"Read it after I'm gone, and call me this time. The number goes to a recorder. Leave a number I can contact you on. Oh, flush the note, Colonel." Black dropped a ten on the counter and walked out the door.

Parks waited for Black to leave and opened the folded napkin. A sudden wave of nausea passed over him as he read it – *Broadway Two Four.*

He called John Black. That weekend, they played a round of golf at Callaway Gardens. They spoke on and off for several hours out on the course, always at a distance from any other players. It seemed Black was a member of a secret portion of the Navy, a sub-set of a SEAL unit dedicated to nuclear weapons as connected with terror groups and ambitious nation states viewed as threats by the Director of National Intelligence.

As part of his duties, Black had spent a great deal of his time researching discrepancies in stockpiles of nuclear material in both peaceful uses, such as power plants, and in weapons assigned to the Department of Defense. His research had uncovered the weapons that had been on that SAC bomber, which had mysteriously been "lost" from SAC's inventory. Apparently, Lemay had done a *good* job of covering up the loss of Broadway Two Four and its payload, but not a *perfect* job.

Black had almost, but not quite, been able to confirm that the loss of the aircraft had occurred on a Chrome Dome mission, not a routine training mission, as all the official documentation had shown.

"As I'm sure you can appreciate, I couldn't just roam around asking questions. I might have eventually been able to find someone who may have known, and who would have admitted the facts, but that would simply have been impractical. Worse, it would have been a nightmare of trying to keep a lid on this problem."

Parks nodded. "I tried, God help me, I tried. It has cost me my career."

"I know. That's why if there was one man that would confirm what I believed, it had to be you. I want to thank you for your honesty. I sincerely hope you and I will never speak of this again."

"Who else will you have to tell?"

"Only one man, the Director of National Intelligence. There will never be anything about this in writing, and your name will not be in my brief to him. All we can do is hope Lemay was right. Wherever Broadway Two Four went down, let's hope it and its crew rest in peace forever."

Until a few moments ago, John Black had been a distant, unpleasant memory, one of many in Martin Parks' life. The email looming before him had brought those memories back in a rush like a cold, winter gale sweeping through the mountains, chilling his very soul.

His hand slowly moved the mouse, planting the cursor over the "open" box. He willed his finger to click it.

The items we discussed some time back have been located. Thought you should know. Attempting to limit damage. Will advise. Do not reply. JFB

"Attempting to limit damage." What did that mean? Black was always an enigma. He even called *himself* John Fucking Black. Parks gazed out the fogged-up window. He had warned Lemay. He had tried to warn the Air Force. The United States of America had stolen his career, his wife and family, and his sanity. It had taken thirty years to ferment and distill the hatred in his brain. It was time to begin his revenge. Colonel Martin Parks would make them pay, every single one of them.

Chapter 16

Office of the Director of Operations
CIA Headquarters, Langley, Virginia
0900 Local Time

The director was wrapping up his morning brief, listening to department heads discussing overnight developments in Europe, Asia, Africa, and any other portions of the world where the Agency had field agents. As Director of Operations, his job differed from the actual CIA Director. His boss answered to the National Security Agency and POTUS. The Operations Director was the individual tasked with actually supervising spies. There was a significant difference.

In his job, James Tidwell made decisions that potentially could cost the lives of agents. As importantly, perhaps, he decided the direction agents would spend their resources and, indirectly, the Agency's money.

As his subordinates completed their summaries of what was happening on foreign continents, Tidwell asked if there were any other items needing the attention of the group.

One of his analysts replied. "Yes, sir, as a matter of fact, there is an item I need to bring to your attention." The speaker was young, seemed inexperienced and bashful.

"Ted, you have the floor," Tidwell stated calmly.

"Well, sir, I understand we have received communication from one of our subcontract agents. She is presently onboard *Atlantis*, the Woods Hole vessel assigned to search for the United airliner recently brought down."

Tidwell leaned forward in his seat. The Agency had quite a number of what they considered "subcontract" employees. In general, these were individuals the CIA had been able to recruit that were in the less-than-obvious areas. They existed not so much as spies, but as eyes and ears in the scientific and college communities. Others were buried deep inside manufacturing and finance.

"So, what did her communications tell us?"

"Our contact indicates they have discovered the wreckage of a B-52 bomber on the ocean floor while searching for the 747."

"An interesting development. I'm sure the guys over at the Pentagon will be fascinated to find something they lost. That's assuming they didn't already know about it." Tidwell leaned back in his chair. He looked around the room, taking inventory of the faces. The subtle nods told him his department heads agreed the information was of little value to the Agency.

Ted cleared his throat. "Director, the agent indicates the aircraft in question has a SAC emblem on the tail, and for reasons she did not elaborate, she is strongly suspicious there are weapons onboard, most likely nukes, sir. I believe this is possibly much more than an interesting historical find. If she is correct, and the wrong people were able to get to the payload…"

The director's entire demeanor changed as Ted's report unfolded. Now he was leaning forward, clenching the pen he had previously been rolling in an absent-minded fashion. His eyes panned around the table. The cool, calm, and slightly smug looks on the other department heads' faces shifted as well. They registered concern. Panic, no. But concern, absolutely. "So, at this time, that's all we know. There *could* be nuclear weapons on board, but our agent on scene doesn't *know* that, correct?"

"Yes, sir, that's absolutely correct."

The director turned to his department heads. "Gentlemen, recommendations?"

There was a brief silence as they all considered the possibilities. Finally, the European head of operations had a suggestion. "Sir, at this point, I don't feel we should go to the DNI with this. Allowing it to get too far up the food chain with incomplete information could blow up in our faces if it turns out to be nothing."

"And the result if we say nothing and it blows up in say, New York?" the director growled. The room was quiet again.

"Sir, a suggestion?" Ted spoke in a quiet tone.

"By all means."

"The bombs, assuming there are any, are on the ocean floor off Greenland. Recovery would likely require the Navy's involvement. There is a segment of a SEAL team tasked with handling situations involving nuclear material in the hands of people we frown on possessing such material. Perhaps we could reach out to them, quietly, and suggest they put together a plan of some sort?"

Heads began to nod around the table.

"Excellent suggestion Mr., pardon me, Ted, you're new here at the table. Your last name again?"

"Cavanaugh, sir."

"Well, Mr. Cavanaugh, you are temporarily assigned to the eighth floor, no longer an analyst. I'll be calling a friend with the Navy, then your boss. You'll be the team leader on this project, and you'll report directly to me. I'll assign some people to you with more experience, but if this turns out to be the real deal, we'll be feeding intel and analysis to the Navy. By the way, how did you manage to place this individual on *Atlantis*?"

"Blind luck sir. She's one of the people I handle. She became available and needed re-assignment. I pulled a few strings and found an option for placing her at Woods Hole just a few weeks ago."

"Well, luck or intuition, in either case, well done. Stay by your phone. As soon as I can organize this, you'll have a small office up here somewhere. You may need to temporarily hand off your other subcontractors temporarily. We'll be in touch." Director Tidwell stood. Ted took it as a signal to take his leave, so he stood as well. The two shook hands, and Ted left the conference room.

Cavanaugh walked back to his cube, unsure whether excitement or fear took precedence in his brain at the moment. As he sat down, a chill of realization hit. This wasn't about him at all.

Chapter 17

Onboard Atlantis

September 17, 0800 hrs local time

Mac and John were seated at the very small table in Mac's cabin. For them to sit, Mac's bed had to be stowed and secured against the wall. The bed and the table both attached to the cabin wall with hinges. One or the other could be folded down, but not both.

The two had just begun to sip their coffee. Neither had more than four hours of sleep following the previous evening's discoveries. Mac had called the meeting between them and Cat before they'd left the ROV trailer last night, actually this morning.

A soft knock on the door indicated Cat had arrived.

"Come in," Mac summoned her. "Good morning, Cat. Have a seat. Coffee?"

"Please," she replied with a weak smile.

Mac stood and poured some of his special blend into a heavy ceramic mug stenciled with some sub's name and number on the side. "Glad you don't mind it black. That's the only way it's served in here."

"Thank you, anyone get any sleep?"

The two men shook their heads.

"Since I called this little meeting, I suppose we should begin. At this point, the only thing I'm positive of is that I alone am who I seem to be. Blackie has always been a dark, mysterious character. God only knows who he's working for right now. You, Miss King, are not what you say you are, and I believe we all have a pretty good idea that a three-lettered agency holds your allegiance. It's just a question of which one. What I do know is, from this moment forward, we all need to be on the same team.

"At this time, *Atlantis* is back in search of an airliner and its black boxes, or at least their location. I believe we all suspect there is a ticking time bomb behind us.

"Let's just open up here and agree on what we think we found last night. John, you first."

Blackie looked at Mac and Cat. "Okay, I answer to the United States of America. Given that, I believe the wreck we looked at a few hours ago is the wreckage of a flight known as Broadway Two Four. That aircraft went down in 1964 with four WA-52 nuclear weapons onboard. I believe I can confirm that soon. Miss King's associate will have processed the photos of the bomber's tail within a few hours I'm sure. Once we have the tail number, the mystery is solved. I have reported what I know right now to an individual that can verify that."

"Cat, what do you have to say?"

"Mr. Black has information that I don't. Given that, I will say that I work with the CIA, and I will confess to the two of you that I have transmitted what I know to my handler with the Agency."

"Christ, she's a spook."

"John, seriously? Are you going to sit here and tell me you didn't know she worked for some alphabet agency? For shit's sake, this is a come-to-Jesus meeting. Okay, let me tell the two of you something you don't know. My IT specialist tells me there were three satellite transmissions off *Atlantis* last night. Two were encrypted, one wasn't. John, you sent an unencrypted message, which I have the text for. I assume you, Cat, sent a message to the CIA. What I need to know is, who sent the other encrypted message?"

Cat and John stared at each other a full half-minute then turned to Mac and nearly simultaneously replied, "I don't know."

"I suspected as much. We have a leak about what the three of us realize is a very serious issue. The leak is possibly critical depending on who the leaker is talking to. Are either of you proficient at encryption or coding? I doubt we have the equipment to crack it, but I'm told there could be hints in the code that might tell us who owns the encryption software."

John shook his head. "Not me."

Cat nodded. "Have your guy send it to me. I'm not an ace, but I might be useful."

"Thank you. One more thing. It may be stating the obvious, but given the time the transmission went out, this individual was almost certainly in the conex last night. That should limit the scope of our investigation.

Be thinking about it. In the meantime, we have an airliner to find."

John and Cat stood, sensing that Mac certainly seemed to be done. They carefully made their way out due to the cramped state of Mac's cabin.

"John, a moment please?" Mac asked.

Black stopped, closed the cabin door once Cat had left, and sat down. "Yes?"

"The individual you emailed, could you explain?"

"Yes. In the simplest terms, he was the only person that would confirm the B-52 we were looking at last night was carrying live ordinance, as opposed to the training mission that was shown on all the official records."

"So, I'm assuming he's not active duty?"

"Correct, he's retired, has been for a few years."

"You're in the covert ops business. Is this individual trustworthy? You've told him a great deal with very few words."

"I suppose you're right, but I wasn't telling him something he didn't already know."

"He knew the what. Now he's aware that we know the *where* as well."

Blackie shook his head. "Obviously you're right. He's been screwed in almost every way possible by the government, but I thought he was entitled to what we found."

"Can we, as in the United States, trust him?"

"Jesus, I hope so. I'm not a conspiracy nut. I don't assume everyone is a possible enemy. But am I one hundred percent sure? I suppose not. I didn't regret sending that email until now, but you're right. I haven't been in touch with him for over ten years. People change. I wish I hadn't sent that email."

"What's done is done."

"Yeah, I guess. Shit, you'd think I would have considered that."

"I suppose, my old friend, the question is, what happens now?"

Chapter 18

Three men riding mules slowly wound their way down a narrow path, a path so narrow a man could span the entire width with his outstretched arms. Thirty hours ago the group had left the town of Peshawar, Pakistan. The group had stopped only three times for a few hours to nap and to rest and water their mules. In the last hour they had passed three well-camouflaged checkpoints staffed by armed men. It was fall, and the altitude and the mountains left the area cold and nearly dark, even though the sun would not set for another hour. The cold had the men, and the guards, wearing layers of robes and pakols, traditional Pakistani men's headgear.

The three passed a tight turn in the worn path, arriving at a curtain of netting covering a stone path so narrow only one man at a time could pass. Guards took the mules away to be fed and watered and beckoned the three to enter the cave complex. Once inside, the three were thoroughly searched and questioned to verify they knew the latest password. Once they met with the guards' approval, they were greeted by smiles and quick prayers to Allah for their successful transit.

A young man wearing spectacles greeted them. "They are waiting for you. Follow me."

The three followed him several hundred meters back into the cave complex. The cave itself appeared to be partially natural. The remainder, as the men had heard from oral histories, had been constructed during the conflict with the Russians before the three were born.

Eventually they arrived in a larger opening some ten meters in circumference. Walls carved out of the native limestone during the conflict with the Russian invaders still showed the signs of picks and manual labor. The floors were covered with rugs. There were a few electric lights, no doubt powered by a generator somewhere. There was a small, low table in the center of the room holding a tea service as well as assorted books and pamphlets.

The group was slightly shocked to see their leader, Usama bin Ladin, seated on a pillow, along with two other, older men they did not recognize. One of them stood.

"Welcome. We see that Allah has blessed your travels to us. We understand you carry important information for our leader."

Arash, the appointed leader of the couriers, bowed and replied. "Yes. We were sent immediately upon our leaders in Peshawar receiving the information. We have been told the information is vital to the cause. The information is in my pouch in the form of a cassette. I was told to guard it with our lives. There is a grenade in the pouch, and I was instructed, if it seemed likely we would be killed or captured, I was to detonate the grenade with the pouch held to my chest."

The associate of bin Laden smiled. "Thankfully, that was not the case, Allah be praised. Please leave the pouch and take some food and rest. You may leave us now." After the couriers had left, there were three left in the cave. Bin Ladin, his head of security, and his technical and scientific advisor. His master of chaos and horror. The man who had developed the plan to send airliners as weapons to the infidels in the United States.

Bin Ladin turned to his head of security. "Our couriers, are we confident of their allegiance?"

"Yes. Arash has been with us for some time. One of his men is a deaf-mute. The third is the son of a man killed by the infidels. They are all to be trusted."

"Very well. You may leave us now." The head of security left with a look of disappointment. Bin Ladin removed the cassette and placed it in a player. He and his scientific advisor listened intently as an associate with access to the internet related new developments. Because of the abilities of the infidels' intelligence gathering abilities, no satellite phones or active internet capabilities were to be found in their new location. They all knew these devices could result in sophisticated bunker-buster bombs dropping out of the sky with no notice.

Any and all communications came to the leaders of Al Queada by means of trusted couriers after having been received in random locations in Pakistan.

The two listened for the fifteen-minute length of the tape. Some years ago, an American infidel had contacted them, indirectly through cut-outs, that the possibility existed that there were American nuclear bombs on the ocean bottom somewhere near Greenland.

Based on that information, and at Bin Laden's demands, a Saudi construction firm had purchased a vessel capable of exploring the ocean bottom, complete with robotic submersibles capable of lifting heavy items from the ocean floor. The ship was originally crewed by Brits, but most had gradually been replaced with immigrants from assorted Arab nations. The ship was an independent business of its own and generally stayed rented often enough and employed in the North Sea oil well business, at a profit. Very few of the crew was aware that a tall man dressed in robes in the mountains of Afghanistan actually owned it.

The tape indicated that the American B-52 bomber had been found, some thirty years after it had been lost, and that the location was now in the hands of the two sitting in the cave. The tape's narrator indicated an independent source had confirmed this information.

Bin Laden's science advisor turned to his employer. "My leader, it would seem to me we have a very real possibility of acquiring one or more of the bombs." The man was thin and wore wire-rim spectacles. His age was hard to determine. Clothed in traditional Saudi robes and headgear, he sat, cross-legged and calm, stroking a scruffy beard flecked with gray.

"Would they still function after thirty years in salt water?"

"Probably not. I doubt we have, or could obtain, the technical expertise to have them function as thermonuclear weapons again, but, Allah be praised, the material itself! It would be very possible to produce a dirty bomb that would render New York uninhabitable for a hundred years, as well as killing possibly one million infidels. Imagine, a million my leader."

Bin Laden pulled on his beard. "Very well. Contact the ship, send an order with the couriers.

Dispatch it to the location. Tell me, is there still a possibility we could enlist our Iranian friends to send assistance?"

"Do you mean would they send one of their diesel subs?"

"That is exactly what I mean. I believe we may need forces capable of taking what we want by force. The infidels will try to stop us once they realize what is happening. Our Iranian allies may not share our objectives, but they desire this material as much as we do. We must form an alliance. You must make this happen, my friend. This will result in a bigger blow to the American devils than our attack in 2001. It may be what we need to force the infidels out of our corner of the world. Make this happen."

"As you say, my leader, it will be done."

Chapter 19

Four days had passed since *Atlantis* had left the location of the B-52. Presently the ship was in the boring phase of any search, mowing the lawn, towing its sonar array, and marking potential targets. So far, there had been no sign of the pings from the acoustic locating devises inside the black boxes.

Mac had spent time today with his engineer reviewing consumables. *Atlantis* was over halfway through its nominal range with respect to fuel and groceries. One of the towed arrays had died, which was hardly a surprise. Repairs had been attempted, but as one might expect, the needed part was not aboard. Some obscure widget not normally prone to failure had expired. A new widget was being FedEx'd to their intended refueling point, a port with the strange name Qaqortoq.

The port certainly lacked a name that rang a bell. On the other hand, all the ports in Greenland seemed to have names that defied spelling, or pronunciation for that matter.

Mac stood and walked the three and a half steps to his coffee pot and refilled his mug. He sat and pondered his much more serious issue, the spy. Between King and Blackie, a short list had been generated. Nathan, his IT guru, had surreptitiously examined every laptop the three on the list had access to. Nathan had eliminated these.

Personally, Mac's favorite was Hameed, but he realized there could possibly be some cultural racism at play. According to Nathan, there had been no new transmissions that were either encrypted or that contained any languages that weren't totally normal.

The crew would probably have been pissed to find out their transmissions to their loved ones, mistresses, and multiple boyfriends had been monitored. Tough shit.

Maddie, MacAdams trusted assistant back at Woods Hole, had provided job applications and any other information she had uncovered on everyone on the list. Nothing had popped out as a red flag. The spy had apparently, as Blackie had termed it, gone deep.

As Mac pondered his issue, there was a knock on his door. "Yes?"

Blackie opened the door and made his way into Mac's cabin. "I have some news, Mac, and I'm afraid it isn't good. Let me rephrase that. I have good and bad news I suppose."

"Okay, I suppose I want the bad news first," Mac replied.

"Thought so. A few moments ago, I had an email, encrypted I would add, that my Navy contacts say there is a vessel headed toward us that our intelligence geeks believe belongs to what some people term as ragheads."

"Excuse me?"

"I'm not trying to be politically incorrect. There is a vessel a few days away from us that has the ability to get down to the wreckage of the B-52 and could also put an ROV down capable of removing certain items from it."

Mac was concerned, seriously concerned. "Seriously? I hadn't even considered that."

"Mac, you're shitting me. You can't believe there were people who would want to get their hands on the payload on the BUFF?"

"Honestly no. I thought this would be a Navy deal all the way. Who else could be coming?"

"Hate to tell you this, but there are entities out there that would love to get their hands on a nuke, or four, even if they are over thirty years old."

"Okay, I get that, now, but how would these entities know? How could they be reacting this quickly?"

"Well, unfortunately, I can't tell you if it's a result of the encrypted email that left *Atlantis* or the one I sent that I deeply regret."

Mac sighed, deeply, and stood and headed for his coffee pot. "Want a cup?" he asked.

"Sure. Vodka seems more appropriate, but what the hell…"

Mac poured two mugs and returned to his seat. "Okay, John, what are our capabilities to stop whoever these people might be?"

"Wow, you went there...okay, probably just me, and possibly you. I think there's also an outside chance that Miss King has some abilities in that area."

"Okay, got it. See the engineer. Much to your surprise, but we do have some, how should I term it, hardware on board. Have a quiet talk with him and see what the picture looks like after your talk. I agree there's a chance that Miss King could possibly be an asset as well. I think we need to have a meeting tonight in the wardroom, excuse me, lounge, to see where we are, agreed?"

"Absolutely. Do I have your approval to discuss the possibility of calling in the cavalry?"

"You do, and I'll tell you why. I wanted to put all that behind me, I believe you do too, but I'll be damned if I'm going to have any of my crew and my techs, who are innocent bystanders, hurt due to the screwed-up situation we're in. We've got very dangerous garbage basically abandoned by people who should have known better thirty years ago causing the circumstances we are faced with. They knew better, damn them."

Blackie stood. "As usual, you're right, my friend. It seems that we will be faced with taking out the trash, again."

Mac stood. The two looked in each other's eyes. Each of them saw things, felt things, that most would never understand. But they knew, only too well. "By the way, what's the good news?"

"I guess I lied. There isn't any. Call me when you want to get together." Blackie quietly smiled, holding up his walkie-talkie.

Chapter 21

Aboard USS Alabama

September 25, 0400 Local Time

The phone beeped in Commander Randall Johnson's cabin. He could see it was the duty officer, the officer currently running the *Alabama* as Commander Randall slept.

The *Alabama* was truly an interesting vessel. She had been launched as a part of the Trident nuclear missile team. Capable of carrying and launching twenty-four nuclear-tipped missiles to targets up to 7500 miles away, the *Alabama* had become redundant due to the SALT agreement with the Soviets.

Each nation had agreed to decrease the number of launchers available in an effort to make the world a slightly safer place. The *Alabama* had briefly been surplus until the Navy made a rather ingenious decision to retrofit the "boat" to a new use. The Navy called all of its subs boats, even though they are larger than many ships belonging to the Navy, and this particular boat had been outfitted to carry a new cargo. It had been reborn and repurposed.

Instead of the twenty-four nuclear-tipped missiles formerly held in the launch tubes, *Alabama* now held twenty non-nuclear cruise missiles and two platoons of SEALs that lived, worked, and exercised in the cavernous compartment taking up the central third of the boat. The four remaining tubes were now capable of allowing the SEALs to enter and leave the boat while it was submerged. The men could take submersible or inflatable delivery vehicles along, these being held in other tubes.

Alabama could now be sent to anywhere on the globe accessible by ocean, carrying powerful and flexible options. The sub still carried the torpedoes that had been part of sub warfare since WWI. In short, *USS Alabama* was capable of carrying a small and violent punch to any situation accessible from the ocean.

Commander Johnson stepped into the wardroom and took his seat at the table. His XO, or Executive Officer, and the navigation officer already occupied their respective seats. A cup of coffee steamed in front of Johnson, along with a file sealed and marked for his eyes only.

Lt. Commander Evans, the XO, gave the short opening brief. "Sir, we received a VLF alert about forty-five minutes ago. According to standing orders, I brought her up to periscope depth, received the message, and went back to 450 meters. The message is decoded and waiting for your directions."

Evans was a good XO and on a career path to be a sub commander, assuming downsizing of the number of available subs didn't freeze him out. Johnson saw Evans as strictly by the book, maybe a little too much so, but perhaps command might bring the ability to see all was not black and white.

Johnson read the message. He was surprised it was from the CNO, the Chief of Naval Operations himself. He had never received a message directly from the CNO. Whatever this message contained, it was out of the norm and being directed at the highest levels.

As soon as he finished the first page of the three-page directive, he handed it to the Navigation Officer.

"Plot a course to that location and give me an ETA. Assume flank speed."

"Yes, sir." The officer took the sheet, stood, and walked to a computer terminal at one end of the room.

"Bring up the display on the big monitor while you're there, Mr. Boyd."

Boyd nodded. Johnson continued reading the orders. He placed the file on the wardroom tabletop and turned to Evans. "As soon as Boyd gives you a course, get on the new heading and go to flank speed. Then I need all the department heads and the SEAL team leader in here in fifteen minutes."

Evans snapped off a salute, nodded, and headed for the control room.

Johnson sat in the wardroom, sipping his coffee and reviewing what his briefing was going to sound like in the upcoming meeting. He turned to the wall where Boyd was working. On the forty-eight-inch plasma display, he could see an icon representing *Alabama* and another blinking square representing their destination.

He watched as he saw *Alabama*'s heading change to a course heading away from their present location, off Gibraltar, toward Greenland. The digital indicators showing depth and speed began to change. As the sub's depth increased, the knot meter reflected a gradual increase from the twelve knots *Alabama* had been cruising at to fifteen then twenty knots. The rate of increase slowed but still climbed to hover in the thirty-knot range.

Alabama was not an attack sub. Her original design, based on mission requirements, had not required speed. Stealth was far more important for a sub carrying nuclear-tipped missiles designed to retaliate against any country that might have made a first strike on the United States. As a result, *Alabama*'s flank speed was slower than that of an attack sub, the "hunter-killers" of the breed.

Even with that, Johnson's nuclear-powered sub could cover large distances faster than most surface ships and could do so with a high degree of stealth.

Johnson turned to Boyd. "What do you see our transit time being right now, Lieutenant?"

"With or without a buffer, sir?" Boyd's question was important. He knew that, under normal protocols, the captain would want to slow to a much stealthier speed about fifty kilometers away from their destination. At flank speed, *Alabama*'s sonar was nearly useless. Water rushing by the sub's passive sonar receivers made them unable to detect another sub or surface ship unless the targets were nearly on top of *Alabama*.

Slowing to a speed under ten knots would allow the sub's sonar equipment and analyst to give its captain a comprehensive picture of anything in the area.

"Assume a thirty-kilometer buffer please."

"In that case, the computer says thirty-seven hours, sir."

Johnson nodded, sipping his coffee. "A day and a half, got it." The door to the wardroom opened, and officers began to filter in. It was time to deliver the most important brief in Commander Johnson's career.

Chapter 22

Commander Johnson sat at his place at the head of the wardroom table. The door was closed, and locked. His department heads and the SEAL team leader were in their places at the table. "Gentlemen, we have just received new mission orders. An American vessel, specifically the civilian oceanographic vessel Woods Hole *Atlantis*, has been searching for the United Airlines aircraft recently downed by an apparent bomb."

"You mean by ragheads," the SEAL commander, Lt. Ragan, interrupted.

Johnson sighed. "Lieutenant, I'm sure you realize that is a politically incorrect, if accurate, term."

Ragan smiled. "Recognized and accepted, sir. My apology, please continue."

"Apology accepted. During said search, *Atlantis* discovered the wreckage of a cold war era B-52. This aircraft, as nearly as can be determined, held four WA-52 nuclear weapons. The issue here is that, according to information provided to the CNO by certain alphabet agencies, hostile elements are aware of the cargo onboard the BUFF. The agency in question is confident there are two vessels on the way to the location of the BUFF, and its cargo. One is a vessel capable of possibly removing those weapons, and the other seems to be an Iranian diesel sub."

"Holy effing shit." Ragan sighed. "So, our assignment is…?"

"Our assignment, gentlemen, is to prevent these people from obtaining the bombs. By any means required."

Ragan seemed thoughtful now. "Sir, could we assume that 'any means required' doesn't mean simply putting torpedoes in the two raghead ships?"

"Lieutenant, as I understand it, my orders consider that possibility as a last resort. Also, for what it's worth, I'm told we have an ex-SEAL on board Atlantis."

"Do we have a name?"

"We do. John Black."

"Holy Christ. Blackie is on *Atlantis*?"

"Affirmative."

Ragan looked pensive. "Well, talk about good news/bad news. He's an obvious choice when it comes to dealing with nukes, on the other hand..."

"Yes?"

"Well, he's John Fucking Black. Need I say more?"

"No, you don't. Here's the bad part, as I see it. Based on present estimates, the two vessels full of bad guys may arrive on site about twenty-four hours before we do. Ragan, my opinion is you should put a plan together assuming it may require boarding *Atlantis* and taking down hostiles while avoiding taking out the crew."

Ragan nodded. "I'd already seen that as a possibility. Sir, is there any way we could go to periscope depth long enough for us to download deck plans for *Atlantis*?"

"We'll arrange it. If it comes to it, I'm assuming you'd want to board at night?"

"Roger that, sir. The good news is that with *Atlantis* being a research vessel, she'll have a low stern. At least we wouldn't have to try to board a freighter with a high deck level. Odds get really shitty trying to sneak up ladders."

"Okay. We'll go to periscope depth ASAP, get your deck plans downloaded, and get back underway at flank speed. My plan is to slow to ten knots about thirty kilometers out, get some idea what the respective positions of the targets are, and then at the time you choose, we'll close on *Atlantis* for your attack."

"Yes, sir, sounds good. One more thing, just to verify. Rules of engagement?"

Johnson thought carefully. His orders from the CNO had only been specific in one regard. Prevent the loss of any nuclear materials to any parties other than the United States. "Lieutenant Ragan, we are collectively in a difficult situation here, but I fully understand your question. Put a plan together that secures the crew of a United States flagged ship and prevent the material from getting into the wrong hands. To that end, use any needed force."

"I get that, sir, but for my men, if we board *Atlantis*, do we shoot first? Or do we fire if fired upon?"

"I have a plan I'm putting together in my head that should simplify that decision for you. You and I will talk just before you leave *Alabama*." Johnson stood. It was an unwritten symbol that the meeting was over. "Let's get to work, gentlemen. Brief your departments. Carry on." The officers surrounding the wardroom table stood and saluted. There was a great deal of work to do.

Chapter 23

Mac, John, and Cat were crowded into Mac's cabin. "Okay, let's regroup. It might be our last opportunity before we get very busy. John, I know you've been in contact with the Navy. What is the status right now as you see it?"

"Okay. From what my sources tell me, the salvage vessel and the Iranian sub are roughly twelve-plus hours away from the site of the BUFF. The cavalry, in the form of the Navy, is about thirty-six hours away, at best. Simply put, we have a twenty-four-hour issue. My question for you, as our mission commander, is, what is our intention during those twenty-four hours?"

Mac leaned back as much as his chair allowed. "Let's think this through. Assuming your information is correct, our unwanted guests will be on station at the B-52 around sundown tonight. We're four hours from that location at present. I'm changing course as soon as we finish this meeting, unless the two of you convince me that I'm wrong."

Cat looked at Mac intently, her chin cradled in her hand, an eyebrow cocked in anticipation. "What are you thinking of doing, Captain?"

"My intention is definitely going to be difficult, but I believe we can pull it off. My opinion is if we attempted to put up a defense using force, we'd be bringing a knife to a gunfight. More importantly, this crew is not going to be harmed if I have any choice in the matter. Our people are a combination of career sailors and students. I *do* intend to slow our opposition down. I have some ideas we need to discuss, and the two of you need to give me your opinions. I do *not* intend to resist them with force."

"What do we need to do?" Blackie asked.

"John, I need you to hide some weapons where we may be able to access them on short notice if required. I need you to meet with the crew and the majority of the scientists and tell them if we're about to be boarded, I want all of them to head for the engineering spaces, and I want the hatches welded shut so they're safe and inaccessible."

Blackie nodded. "Sound advice, sir. I can do that."

"Cat, how far can *Atlantis* be from the bomber and still have Homer capable of reaching the wreck?"

King looked at Mac, a cryptic smile beginning to show on her face. "What do you have up your sleeve, sir?"

"As I said, my intention is to slow them down. I'm assuming they're going to arrive on station over the BUFF and tell us to stay the hell out of their way, at least I hope that's how it goes down. If we were a mile or so away, and if Homer were lying on the bottom, when they sent an ROV down to try to extract the weapons from the B-52, Homer might run over to the wreck and cut the umbilicals..."

Kat smiled. "Sneaky as shit, sir. I like it."

"Here's the problem. I think we agree someone that was in the conex when we found the B-52 is a traitor. I need you to tell me the absolute minimum number of your team you would need to pull this off. I need their names as well. Further, I need you to get the riggers to fit Homer with a grapple and cutter arm."

"Sir, just a suggestion, but while we're doing that, I think we should put a coat of black spray paint on Homer, just in case the opposition goes to looking around."

"Excellent suggestion. Now, who do you need as a minimum to pull this off?"

Cat considered the question, and she finally answered. "Sir, I've absolutely got to have Evan. He's positively the best pilot for Homer, no question about it. I really need Karen as well. From the standpoint of optics, she's the bomb. Oops, bad phraseology. Nonetheless, she knows more about the camera capabilities than any of the rest of us."

Mac paused, considering the options. "I need you to find a way to put them on standby without telling them what I have in mind. I need you to compartmentalize the plan. Can you get Homer in position just dealing with Evan and the riggers? And can you put Karen on standby without her knowing our objective?"

"I would never try something like this under normal circumstances, but I think I can find a way to do what you're asking. If it wasn't so important, I'd tell you to kiss my ass. I don't care for lying to my people. In this case, I get it. One hundred percent."

"I haven't asked you this question yet. Since you're working for the Agency, do you know anything more I need to be aware of?"

"Hmm, in all honesty, I might be considered a spook, but I'm not an agent. My assignments, as long as I've worked for the Agency, have been to observe and report to my handlers. With a few exceptions, that I'm obviously not free to discuss, I've never taken on what you might call an active operation. In short, I haven't been told what the Agency is doing with the information I've been supplying. What I suspect has happened in this case is that someone at the Agency picked up a phone and spoke to someone like the CNO. Together, they put together a plan, and that is where we are right now."

Mac nodded. "Actually, that's exactly my impression as well. Tell me, and be honest, what do you think the people in the vessels headed our way are going to do? At this point, my biggest concern is for the crew on *Atlantis*. Should I just plot a course for Greenland and leave the bombs to them? John, I'd appreciate your input here as well."

Cat looked at Mac then turned to John. "I'm assuming you've been in a similar circumstance. I haven't. I defer to you."

John Black sipped his coffee. "Captain, I'm afraid there's really no middle ground. Okay, I get it about not trying to take them on head-to-head. What you're left with is either be sneaky and try to discreetly delay them or cut and run. It's black or white. The only way to positively rule out any chance of the crew being harmed is to set a course for Greenland right now.

"To answer your question, while they certainly have the ability, I just don't think they would just sink us with no warning. Tactically, it doesn't benefit them to board us unless they need something we have. That being said, those are the logical options. Will they be logical? Who knows. Honestly, anything except running entails risk. I'm afraid it's your call, Mac."

Mac leaned back, deep in thought. "Very well. My mind is made up. This is terribly important. If it didn't potentially involve the possibility of a case of nuclear terrorism at the highest levels, I wouldn't even hesitate. We delay them. John, proceed with hiding the weapons. Cat, proceed with putting your team together. We have twelve hours, more or less. Let's use it wisely." Mac stood, the unwritten signal that the meeting was over. Cat and John nodded and left the room.

He stood and walked to his coffee pot and warmed his mug. *I hope I'm doing the right thing.*

Chapter 24

Onboard Atlantis

1800 hrs

Mac sat in the captain's chair on the bridge. *Atlantis* was holding position with her thrusters about one mile off the location of the wreckage of the B-52. Homer was resting on the ocean floor about two hundred meters away from the wreckage with his new coat of flat black paint. Presently Cat and her team were killing time. They weren't even in the conex trailer.

Under her and John's direction, she and Evan had placed the ROV in position and powered it down. Homer was ready to interfere with an attempt to salvage the nukes on the B-52, as was Cat's team, but at present they were waiting.

Mac watched *Atlantis*'s radar as it swept the surface on a fifty-mile range. The radar showed a ship approaching. Mac, and everyone else on the bridge, knew the identity of the approaching green blip on the screen.

John and Cat had completed their respective tasks. John had collected and hidden some handguns in places he deemed appropriate. Cat had placed *Atlantis's* ROV in position to interfere with any attempt to remove the deadly cargo from the BUFF. Everything was ready, in theory, for the approaching threat. Speaking of John and Cat, at the present time, they were missing. That was unusual.

Atlantis was equipped with state-of-the art communications equipment on the bridge. So, Mac was not surprised to hear a message coming across the VHF radio. The scanner on the bridge lit up on channel 13, the accepted hailing frequency for ship-to-ship communications.

"Captain *Atlantis*, this is Captain *Salvage One* calling, over."

The helmsman turned to Mac. "Do we reply?"

"No. Wait. Let them get impatient."

"Yes, sir."

"So, John Fucking Black, I remember why you acquired that nickname." Cat leaned back in her cot, pulling a sheet over her nude body. "Is this how you usually blow off steam before an op?"

"It depends."

"On what?"

"On how much time I have and how interesting my companion might be. There isn't a lot of time, so I guess you could assume you're interesting as hell."

Cat grinned. "There's a lot of stress involved here. For your information, this is stress relief for me."

"Call it what you will. We both know this doesn't mean anything, and that's a pity, but it's the truth, isn't it? Want to know the best part?"

"I can hardly wait..."

"From my experience, normally anything involving the CIA means someone like me gets screwed. At the present time, I'm screwing the CIA."

"Past tense, JFB. You screwed the CIA. You'll have to show me more to do it again. I've had better."

Blackie pulled the sheet away and administered a hard slap to Cat's ass. "As have I. We'll have to try this again after this deal is done. Do I qualify for a re-run?"

"Possibly." She threw the sheet aside and stood, turning her stern toward John. She pulled a robe around herself and sat in the one chair in the stateroom. She looked at Blackie. "What is this, John? What are we doing now? I assume this won't become anything, and I'm fine with that, but why me?"

"You're the only woman onboard that understands people like me. You're more like me than you want to admit. I can see it in your eyes. You've seen things that nice, normal people shouldn't have to see. We see the world differently, you and I. So does Mac. He's put it behind him better than most, but it's still there. Besides, I noticed that sexy librarian vibe you were sending as soon as you came onboard."

King simply nodded. She stood and dropped her robe. She pulled a plastic container off the desk, popped the top, and pulled out a towlette. She tossed the container to Black. "Pre-moistened wipes, no private showers. We need to get cleaned up and return to the bridge before anyone catches on."

Blackie grinned. "We should be safe. I have a feeling most people think we can't stand to be around each other."

"That's because it's true. You're an unmitigated asshole, Blackie, always will be."

He laughed. "Glad we understand each other, bitch." He extended his hand.

She shook it and smiled. "Right. Hurry up. Get dressed and get the hell out of my cabin before my roomie comes back."

John did as he was told and was about to make his exit.

"John, come back in a moment."

"Yes?"

"Have you told Mac we were on an op together in the past?"

"No, have you?"

"No. Should we?"

"I don't think so. There's no reason to do so. As far as I can see, it has no bearing on this mission. Up to you though."

Cat hesitated. "I suppose you're right. Leave, now. Okay?"

He nodded and left quietly.

John walked onto the bridge.

"Where have you been?" Mac asked.

"I caught a power nap. What's up?"

"We were hailed ten minutes ago by a vessel calling itself *Salvage One.* I decided to let them stew awhile. Any thoughts?"

Before Black could reply, the radio lit up again. "Captain *Atlantis*, Captain *Salvage One* calling, over."

Blackie nodded. "I'd say go ahead."

"*Atlantis* copies, go ahead."

"Captain MacAdams, we both know why we are here. Please maintain your position and do not interfere if you do not want to be destroyed. Do you understand?" The voice had a British accent, but there seemed to be an undercurrent Mac couldn't quite pick out.

"*Atlantis* copies." Mac turned to Blackie. "I'm going to leave it at that for now, unless…?"

"No, sounds good to me." John nodded.

About that time, Cat walked on the bridge. "Sorry, sir, what's our status?"

Mac slowly pulled his long frame from his chair and walked to the port side of the bridge. He pointed off to the north, into the prematurely dark skies. "Those lights you see are the salvage ship. The sub is likely laying on the surface, hiding behind the salvage ship. Just before you came in, they hailed us on the VHF radio telling me, by name, I might add, to stay put or be destroyed."

"So, it's begun; and the Navy, how long...?"

"Roughly twenty-four hours."

Mac turned back to John. "I realize it's not really your area of expertise, but what are your thoughts about what they can do in twenty-four hours?"

"Maybe we should continue this conversation in the wardroom?"

Mac sighed. "I suppose." He nodded toward the door leading off the bridge.

The three re-convened in the lounge.

"The way I see it, the tail broke off at some point. That means there's only one bulkhead between them and the bomb bay. With no concerns for the wreck's integrity, conceivably they could drag a weapon or two out in twelve hours or so. What are you thinking, Mac?"

MacAdams nodded. "I think I agree. In a research setting, we'd spend days photographing the wreck then cutting the bulkhead, so probably a week. Different deal altogether. The difference between archaeology and strip mining I suppose."

He looked across the table at John and Cat. "I know you might not be able to answer, but in your opinions, when is the ideal time to wake Homer up and try to ruin their day?"

Cat looked at Mac then John. "Not my area. We can have Homer ready with twenty minutes notice. John?"

"I'm going to assume they figure the U.S. is going to try to stop them. That's the main reason I assume they brought the sub. They had to know the surface ship would be a sitting duck for several days at least. Given that, they'll be in a big hurry. I can't tell you how long they'll need, but I think I can tell you how we'll know."

"Yes?"

"We just watch them. They're what, a mile or so away? We simply put people on deck with binoculars. I realize it's dark, but they'll have to use deck lights. When they start getting a crane ready, we turn Cat loose."

Mac grinned. "I thought along those lines. It just seemed too simple. Okay, let's get to work."

Chapter 25

Onboard Atlantis
ROV Lab 2330 hrs

Cat's crew sat in their positions at the controls for Homer in the ROV trailer. Homer still lay on the ocean floor as an inactive piece of hardware. Cat was seated in the center chair, Evan, Homer's pilot, to her right, Karen, the lighting and photographic expert, to Cat's left. Mac and John stood behind them.

They had been somewhat surprised by the actions of *Salvage One*. The salvage ship had deployed a manned submersible. In a way, it made sense. A manned vessel could make more progress than an ROV, at least one the size of Homer. On the other hand, a manned sub had a shorter amount of bottom time. The submersible they had seen set off the stern of the salvage vessel a mile or so away was large, larger than anything Woods Hole had.

Taken in context, however, a commercial salvage ship wasn't interested in research or observation. The intent in this case was to rip out the bulkhead separating the bombs from their resting place and to attach a lifting cable to a bomb, or bombs.

The group in the ROV trailer had an idea of what was going on at the location of the B-52, but that was all. Homer was presently inactive, and even if he had been powered up, he was too far away. Unless he had been a lot closer and using his lights, the group in the trailer on *Atlantis* had no idea what was actually happening on the bottom of the sea.

Cat turned to Mac, a question mark on her face. He nodded.

She swiveled to Evan. "Power Homer up. Go through your diagnostics, but do not turn on lights or sonar."

Evan looked at her, nodded, and began typing on his keyboard. Cat had told Evan and Karen the least she could and still have them sufficiently informed to do what was needed.

Mac stood in the back of the room, more or less aside John and behind Karen.

A little more than fifteen minutes later, Evan turned to Cat. "What's next, boss? Homer is ready to go."

"Okay. Head toward the wreck. I need you to be two to three hundred feet up off the bottom"

"What am I going to be looking for?"

"You're going to be looking for a cable or rope."

"I'll never see it without some lights, boss."

"I know. Once you're within fifty feet of the wreck, and at least two hundred feet off the bottom, you can turn on your lights. Absolutely no sonar though, got it?"

"Got it. Assuming I find a rope, cable, or whatever, what do I do then, boss?"

"You grab it and cut it, Evan."

"What?"

"Evan, there are weapons on the B-52. Nukes. People with bad intentions are trying to grab them. We have to stop them. Do we understand each other?"

"Hell yes, boss." Evan turned to his joysticks and peered at his monitor, looking at his depth gauge and looking at his plot of the ocean floor to see where Homer was in relation to the wreck.

Mac shifted from foot to foot, tension building in his body as he watched the proceedings. Evan's seeming eagerness to ruin the plans of the opposition made Mac breathe a sigh of relief. Evan wasn't the mole.

Cat had a plan that would meet Mac's intentions to delay the actions of the enemy. This might just work. He watched the monitors with interest. One suddenly lit up after Evan pushed a key on his keyboard. Mac could plainly see a yellow nylon or poly-looking cable in the screen.

"I've got a cable in sight, boss."

"I see it too. Cut it, now."

"Evan, stop right now unless you want me to scatter Cat's brains all over you!"

Mac looked at Karen; he was in shock. Karen had pulled a small pistol from somewhere and was holding it less than a foot from Cat's head. Mac tried to remember, where in the trailer had John said he hid a pistol? And would it do any good? He and John were both three or four feet from Karen and Cat. All Karen had to do was pull the trigger.

Mac watched, frozen in place. Evan backed away from the console and his keyboard and controls, holding his hands up.

"Sure, Karen, whatever you say. Don't shoot anyone, okay?" Mac had never felt more helpless in his life.

"You people are fools," Karen said quietly, a sneer crossing her face. "As we sit here, a team of fighters is about to board this silly vessel. All of your Ph.D.'s will never stop us from achieving our goals. Once we have this material, we will be able to kill millions of your infidels. Our—"

Karen's speech was interrupted by a flash of motion on Cat's part that occurred so quickly Mac could hardly take it all in. Karen had made an amateurish mistake. She may have had a gun only six inches from Cat's head, but she was easily within the reach of her intended victim.

Mac was only three or four feet from the two women, but as he made an attempt to respond, he also saw John moving out of the corner of his eye. The action before him happened so fast his brain could hardly process it. Cat's hands flew in a manner Mac vaguely recalled from his stint in Aikido training. Cat's left arm made a sweep, diverting Karen's right hand and, more importantly, the gun, away from Cat's head.

A move of Cat's right hand toward the gun hand might have ended the problem but for one thing; Cat was seated in a chair on rollers. A move Cat might have practiced a hundred times from a standing position and, from what Mac could see, might have actually used in reality, didn't work as intended.

The gun stayed in Karen's hand longer than it should have by probably a half-second. Exactly long enough for Karen's index finger to pull the trigger.

The gun went off with a huge report in the tight quarters of the trailer. By now, Cat had two hands on Karen's forearm. Out of the corner of his eye, Mac saw Blackie grab his abdomen in pain as he was blown backwards by the single round that escaped from

Karen's weapon. In the entire second and a half it took for all of this to transpire, Mac had been moving to dive into the fray.

He was too late. Once Cat saw that John had taken a round, she visibly shifted into another state. In the blink of an eye, one of her hands held Karen's wrist, and the gun, toward the ceiling. With her other hand, Cat grabbed the same pen she always twirled in one hand from the desk and buried it in Karen's eye, traveling at least five inches into the woman's brain. Karen died within seconds. Strangely, Mac had the impression this wasn't the first time Cat had done something like this.

"Evan, do what Mac said, now!" Cat spun around in her chair, turning toward John. "How bad is it?"

John Black sat slumped on the floor, his back leaned up against an equipment rack. By now, Mac and Cat were kneeling on either side of him. "Not good guys, not good. Roll me over and tell me if there's an exit wound."

Mac did as he was asked. "No, no exit."

"Didn't think so. If we were in a city with a trauma center, I might have a chance. No way out here. Just a matter of time."

Just then, Mac's radio crackled to life. "Captain, we've got two launches approaching. Looks like about a dozen of them, loaded for bear." It was the chief engineer, in effect Mac's second-in-command.

Mac pushed the push-to-talk button. "Copy that. Go with the plan. Sound the collision alarm and head everyone to the engineering spaces and go into lockdown mode." The engineer had briefed with Mac and John on the plan. The collision alarm went off, bells ringing all over *Atlantis*. Mac turned back to John. "What can we do for you, John?"

Black pulled his sweatshirt up. "Patch me up. Duct tape over the wound then wrap gauze around it. My 9mm is on top of this rack behind me. Wrap it into the gauze and let me lie here. Stop the ragheads, you two. Cut that line and then sit back and do what the bad guys say."

Mac nodded. He and Cat went to work patching Blackie up as well as possible. As he and Cat worked on John, he turned to Evan. "Can you see the cable?"

Evan was shaken, obviously, but he turned to his monitors. "No, sir, not right now, but I'll find it."

Cat stripped some duct tape off a roll and applied it to Blackie's abdomen. Without looking away from her work, she calmly addressed Evan. "Find it and cut it. It's vital, Evan. People will die if we can't screw these people up, got it?"

"Yes, ma'am. You can count on me." He gazed at his monitor as he directed Homer to pan back and forth.

Mac ran his hand across the top of the equipment rack until he located the pistol John had referred to. He handed it to Cat as she began to wrap gauze around Black.

She held the Beretta up and opened the slide far enough to verify a round was chambered. She flipped the safety to the off position and pulled the hammer back. "Okay, you're locked and loaded. Where do you want me to put it so you can get to it?"

John pointed to a spot on the right side of his abdomen. "Right here. Try to arrange the gauze so if I've passed out one of you can reach it. Remember, guys, we only have to hold them off until the cavalry gets here."

Mac nodded. "We'll take it from here, John. Get some rest. Are you in pain? Should I find some morphine?"

"My old friend, you and I both know a gut shot is the worst. If you can get some juice, shoot me up, but right now, worry about our raghead friends, okay?"

Evan interrupted the concentration on Black. "Guys, I have the cable in sight again. Cut it?"

"Yes, immediately," Cat replied, never taking her eyes off Blackie as she finished the wraps.

"Done," Evan replied a few seconds later.

Cat turned to Mac. "What now, Captain?"

"I recommend we back off a little and power down."

"Do it," she snapped to Evan. "Shut Homer down as soon as possible."

Evan nodded and got busy on his controls.

The group could hear men tromping around and talking outside. Moments later a group of men pulled the door open on the conex. The leader, a bearded man with a bad attitude and an AK-47, entered the trailer.

"Back away from the controls. Which of you is in charge?"

Chapter 26

Onboard U.S.S. Alabama

Commander Johnson and Lieutenant Ragan sat alone in the wardroom. Johnson looked at the monitor and turned to Ragan. "Lieutenant, we're about six hours away from being on station including some reconnaissance time. Do you have a boarding option planned yet?"

"Yes, sir. We're going to put two inflatables with six men each as close as we feel comfortable. The teams will go over the side and swim the last leg. A third inflatable will be about one hundred meters astern of *Atlantis* with two snipers with night scopes and a spotter. Do we have an estimate of what sea conditions are on the site?"

"The navigator is saying indications are nearly calm."

Ragan grinned. "Excellent. When the swimmers signal, anyone on the stern that doesn't look like an obvious *Atlantis* crew member will be neutralized, and then the swimmers will board. They'll be loaded for bear and shoot first and ask questions later. I'll need weapons release and authorization from you before that happens, sir."

"You've had an opportunity to study the deck plans?"

"Yessir, I just hope MacAdams has done what he should have. Hopefully he has the crew sequestered in the engineering spaces and we won't get confused about who the bad guys are. That's S.O.P. for a vessel being boarded by pirates. By the way, you had mentioned you had a plan that would help us?"

Johnson stood and walked to the display on the wall. Entering a few keystrokes, he changed the display to simply show *Atlantis*, the salvage vessel, and the sub in a radius of about three nautical miles. "My plan is to approach from here"—pointing to the far side of *Atlantis*, away from the opposition— "and offload your team at periscope depth. I'd like you to put someone on the bridge to look at the periscope and give you a last-minute peek at what they see going on aboard *Atlantis*."

Ragan nodded. "Sounds good, next?"

"Then *Alabama* will sneak away and go deep. How long will you need to be in a position to board? Maximum."

"Give me fifteen minutes."

"Very well then. Start a countdown clock when you see *Alabama* submerge. Fifteen minutes later we're going to do an emergency blow right between the two vessels. Showy as hell, broaching a hundred feet of hull out of the water. I'll have men firing flares, the bullhorns blaring that the U.S. Navy is here, yada-yada…"

"Love it, sir, nothing stealthy about *that* plan, but it will make for a superb cover to board."

"That was my intent. After that, I'm afraid it's on you, Lieutenant."

"Understood, sir. Let me go brief the men."

"Absolutely. Good hunting, Lieutenant. By the way, consider this as your weapons release." The two stood and shook hands. Things would get very interesting sometime in the next six hours or so.

Chapter 27

Mac sat on the floor of the bridge, surrounded by men from the assault force of the salvage vessel. The last few hours had been trying, but so far, nothing terrible had taken place. *Atlantis* had been boarded by a motley crew of what Mac considered pirates. The fact that they had a political reason for their actions changed nothing in his mind.

The men, mostly bearded, all heavily armed, and some who spoke English, had been expected. They had entered the conex shouting and demanding to speak to the captain. Mac had indicated that would be him. They had forcefully removed Cat and Evan from their places at the control console and held them, two men holding each.

The boarders had been confused to find John Black leaning against an equipment rack, obviously injured, and a deceased Karen sprawled in her chair with a pen embedded in her eye.

At the time the group took over the conex, the odor of gunpowder still hung in the air and Karen's small pistol lay on the floor. The pirate's apparent leader had spent some minutes on a walkie-talkie speaking to someone in what sounded like Arabic to Mac.

A fifteen-minute exchange followed. The "pirate" leader, a bearded man that introduced himself as "Michael" asked, with a British accent, where the crew might be. Mac replied that the crew was sequestered at his instruction in the engineering spaces and were not coming out under any circumstances for twenty-four hours regardless of what they were told.

"And if I threated to shoot this young woman"— pointing a large pistol at Cat— "what will you do then?"

"I will tell you to shoot her, me, or anyone in this room. It will not change their minds. You must understand, my crew is not military. They are a mixture of career sailors and students. They should be spared any injury. That is my position, and no action on your part will change my mind in this regard."

"Captain, you were instructed not to interfere with our task, under penalty of the destruction of this vessel. Yet, within the last few moments, you and these people"—waving his pistol at Cat and Evan— "have cut the line we intended to use to lift the weapons to the surface."

"In my book, that is excellent news. They did as ordered, in spite of an attempt by a traitor we were unaware of," he stated, pointing at Karen's corpse. "I take responsibility for their actions, and I ask that you hold me, and not my crew, at fault here."

Michael shook his head. "All moot points, Captain MacAdams. When the cable your people cut fell into the wreckage, that cable fowled the props on our manned submersible. We have two men trapped and a matter of hours from dying due to your actions. My leader has instructed me to command your people to use your robot to free them, or I'm to start executing them one at a time."

Mac hesitated, taking all this in. After consideration, he answered. "Michael, I realize your leader probably doesn't see it this way, but I ask you to consider what I ask. I will direct the ROV operators to follow your orders to the best of their ability in exchange for humane treatment on my wounded crew member and my crew as a whole. We have no desire for your men to die."

"What are you asking?"

"Can you have John here moved to my bunk? If you have someone trained medically, will they render any possible aid and administer morphine? If you'll do that, I'll instruct Miss King and Evan to do everything they can to free your submersible."

Michael was in a position of having to consider his options. He got back on his portable radio for another long conference with someone on what Mack assumed was the large salvage ship. After the conversation, he turned to Mac. "We agree to your conditions, for now." He barked some orders to his men. "Accompany me to the bridge, Captain MacAdams. I assume you have a stretcher somewhere aboard?"

"Yes, of course. I'll show you where it is on the way." Turning to Cat, he spoke quietly. "Miss King, I'm directing you and Evan to do your very best to free their submersible as quickly as possible."

Cat nodded, as did Evan. "Yes sir. Michael, will you please ask your men to release us?"

Michael did so.

Mac turned to look at his old friend. John was pale and had not spoken during the entire exchange with the pirates. For some reason, Mac suspected Blackie was playing possum; at least Mac hoped that was the case.

Now, nearly four hours later, Mac sat on the floor of the bridge. There seemed to have been some degree of success freeing the pirates' submersible, but Evan and Cat had not been brought to the bridge. Mac had no clue where they were or what they were doing. An hour or so ago, Michael had spun around in his, actually Mac's, chair and pointed his finger at him.

"Where is your Navy? I'm sure you have contacted them. No doubt there are already aircraft orbiting at some very high altitude to protect their bombs. Don't worry, we have a plan for that."

"I'm sure you do. I know the Navy is on the way. My friend John has been in touch. Do you see anything on the radar?" There was no point in lying, although John saw no reason to tell them everything he knew.

Michael stood and walked to the radar. "No, the only ship within one hundred miles appears to be a freighter moving seventy miles to the south." About that time, Michael's portable radio went off with the sound of Arabic being spoken in an exciting, rapid-fire mode. Michael turned to Mac.

"Great news! With the help of your people and your little toy robot, the bombs are secured and we are ready to begin lifting. Allah be Praised!"

"Congratulations, Michael. In all honesty, the only thing I'm happy about is the fact that our people were able to prevent the crew of your submersible from dying. I hope you'll keep that in mind when you consider how Miss King and Evan are treated. While we're on the subject of treatment of my crew, I appreciate your having someone setting up an IV and morphine for John."

"Captain MacAdams, while I have little respect for any infidel, your concern for your crew and associates is admirable. So you know, we understand that your Navy will likely be on site at any time. That's why, once the weapons of mass destruction presently being lifted from the sea floor, they will be transferred to our submarine. I have little doubt that our salvage vessel will be destroyed by your country's military. I feel certain that, within hours, I will be dead. But I will be a martyr. Allah will reward me and my crew."

"Michael, you and I will have to agree to disagree on how our Gods will reward us for what we do in this life. My life is quite simple. I want to be comfortable with what I do every day and how I have treated those I encounter. God bless you. Can you please bring Miss King and Evan to the bridge when you are done with them?"

Michael seemed somewhat disturbed. He hesitated. "You are correct, MacAdams. We will have to disagree, but I see no reason to deny your request." He pulled out his radio and gave instructions to someone in Arabic. "Your people will be brought to the bridge soon."

Mac had assumed his seat on the floor again, his back leaned against the rear bulkhead of the bridge next to the passageway leading to his cabin and the wardroom. Michael and one of his men were the only other people on the bridge. The bridge itself was dark, lit primarily by the displays and instruments. The scene out the wraparound bridge windows was quite dark as well. The seas were nearly slick calm, lit by a half moon overhead. About a mile away, out the port windows, the lights on the salvage vessel were bright, casting a reflection on the slick, cold waters of the North Atlantic.

Footsteps on the port bridge wing signaled the arrival of Cat and Evan, accompanied by four armed guards. Mac stood and walked toward them. He looked them over, searching for any sign the two had been abused in any physical way. Seeing no sign of any abuse, he smiled. "Nice to see you two. How are you?"

Cat sighed and gave a near smile. "Okay, I guess. We're just tired. It's been hard work. First, Evan cut away the cables trapping their submersible, and then we were told to reconnect the lifting cable to the two bombs."

Evan spoke up. "We're sorry, Mac. I know you didn't want that, but you *did* tell us to cooperate."

"No, no. It's fine. As a whole, *Atlantis* has done all we can. I agreed to these conditions for your safety and Michael's promise to help John's condition. He's fulfilled his part of the deal."

"How is John?" Cat asked.

"He's resting quietly in my bunk."

Michael spoke up. "My men rigged a saline IV bag and administered morphine. We found the pistol of course. All of you were wise not to take any direct action. Just because we are what your country would consider terrorists, we see no need to harm any of you. Provided you do not interfere with my mission, I see no reason to kill. Your ship and your crew will be hostages to guarantee our safety until we can escape." Michael gave a smug grin.

Cat looked at Michael and Mac. "Can I see John?"

"Of course, in my opinion."

Michael nodded curtly.

Cat turned and walked off the bridge.

Three minutes later, it started.

Chapter 28

Off the stern of Atlantis

One hundred fifty meters off the stern of *Atlantis,* a black inflatable bobbed in the nearly calm waters. Onboard, two SEAL snipers with .300 Win Mag rifles, equipped with suppressors and infra-red laser scopes, eyed the three pirates on *Atlantis'* stern. One was on each corner, port and starboard, and one had a position on the raised gantry that held the ship's crane.

Each held an AK-47 at the ready. The SEALs in the inflatable could clearly see the enemy in the bright deck lights illuminating the stern and out about fifty meters. The good news for the snipers and their spotter was that they were one hundred meters past what the lights illuminated and that the bright lights absolutely killed the ability of the enemy to see them.

The two snipers settled into a rhythm watching the dots in their scopes dance up and down slowly on their targets, anticipating the sight picture needed when they would actually pull the trigger.

Two teams of six men each bobbed in the water, ready to board *Atlantis* as soon as *Alabama* made her dramatic entry on scene. A series of flashes with an infra-red flashlight had told the spotter, and the snipers, that they were ready and waiting. Once the party actually started, the violence that SEALs trained day and night to deliver with precision would begin.

On the Bridge of Atlantis

Even from a half-mile away, an 8000-ton submarine broaching the surface at a near forty-five-degree angle and traveling thirty miles per hour was an impressive site. It may have been several hours before sunup, but between the moonlight and the lights on the salvage vessel a mile away, the show was quite impressive.

All at one time, Mac heard excited voices on Michael's portable radio in Arabic combined with pretty impressive radio traffic on the conventional VHF radio that all ships monitored as a call channel.

"Break, break, break. This is *USS Alabama*. Be advised that any, repeat any, threat to U.S. vessel *Atlantis* will result in immediate destruction of vessels causing such damage."

The announcement by *Alabama* was then repeated in Arabic.

Michael scowled at Mac and picked up the microphone for the VHF radio. "This is *Atlantis*. We are holding the crew hostage. Explosives have been planted. Any action on your part will result in the death of the crew of *Atlantis*. Do not test us." Michael threw the microphone down. "Shut off the radio," he yelled to one of his men.

Mac realized that the situation was going to change significantly at any moment and that there was absolutely nothing he could do about it. In a very real sense, he was glad that Cat wasn't on the bridge right now.

Michael issued orders, in Arabic, and quickly his men took up positions next to Mac and Evan. The men immediately put pistols to Mac's and Evan's heads. "Captain MacAdams, I make no apology. You and your crew are my safety net. If your Navy makes any attempt to—"

Suddenly there were muffled sounds outside the bridge. Small tinkling noises of breaking glass interrupted Michael's words.

Mac felt a sudden shot of warm liquid spray his face as the head of the guard holding a gun to him exploded with a sickening crunch. To Mac's amazement, the man holding Evan hostage suffered a similar fate. Seconds later men dressed in wet suits wearing black, tiger-striped makeup and night vision goggles, entered both sides of the bridge.

"Place your hands in the air. Navy SEALs are assuming command of *Atlantis*. Any movement will be seen as a threat. Is Captain MacAdams present?"

Mac nodded. "I'm MacAdams."

"Captain, identify anyone that's a part of your crew on the bridge, sir."

Mac pointed at Evan. "He's part of my crew, and two more members are in my cabin back there." Mac pointed at Michael. "He's Michael, the apparent leader of the pirates."

The SEAL looked at Michael. "Sir, I recommend you and anyone under your command hit the fucking deck with your hands behind your head unless you have a death wish."

Michael muttered something in Arabic, and his men slowly assumed prone positions on the deck. More SEALs in wet suits flooded onto the bridge and began frisking the pirates.

As Mac stood on the increasingly crowded bridge, he heard Michael's portable radio blare what sounded like a highly excited voice calling in Arabic. The SEAL team leader nodded to one of his men. The SEAL walked over to Michael's radio and picked it up. He keyed the mike and spoke in an authoritative voice, in Arabic.

The SEAL team leader knelt down next to Michael. "My translator just informed your people the shit has hit the fan, Michael. My team has found and disarmed your explosives. All of your men, other than these few"—he waved his hand across the bridge—

"are on their way to meet Allah. If your ship, or the piece-of-shit Iranian sub over there, even flinch, *Alabama* will send everyone to meet Allah as well. If you want to see them live, get on the radio now and tell them to surrender. Your call."

Michael turned his head, sneering at the SEAL team leader. "By now the weapons of your country are aboard the sub and will be leaving the scene."

"Keep thinking that, dude." The team leader paused and held a throat microphone. "*Atlantis* is secure. Ragheads are telling me the package is being loaded on the sub." His face registered concentration as he listened to a reply through his earpiece. "Copy that, will do." Turning to MacAdams, he asked, "Captain MacAdams. Can we speak in private?"

"Of course, this way please." Mac lead the SEAL team leader back to the lounge. As he passed his cabin, he stuck his head in the door.

"How is he?"

Cat shook her head. "Unconscious. I don't think he has long."

The SEAL asked, "Can I help?"

"I have a crew member with a gut shot. If you can help, please do. He's an old friend, and an ex-SEAL as well."

"Blackie? It's John?"

Mac nodded.

"Get me a medical team and all their gear to the bridge, NOW!" he said into his radio. Then he gestured for Mac to proceed.

The two entered the lounge. The SEAL closed the door behind him. "Captain, is there anything else I can do to help you or your crew? *Atlantis* is secure. The captain of the *Alabama* wants to get them out of the engineering spaces just in case. My team hasn't been able to get them to come out."

"Just in case of what, exactly?"

"Well, I'm assuming you realize the ragheads have a sub with them. The captain can't rule anything out. He's concerned they may fire a torpedo at *Atlantis*, *Alabama*, or both. It will, of course, be a suicidal act, but these guys have proven over and over they aren't controlled by logic. He believes he can decoy their fish, but he doesn't want your crew trapped below."

"Very well, let's go get them out now." Mac stood and walked out the door with the SEAL team leader in tow. As he walked through the bridge, he passed three SEALs unzipping large waterproof bags of what looked like medical equipment. He paused long enough to nod at them and tell them, "Take good care of Blackie."

"We will, sir." One nodded and headed toward Mac's cabin with a serious look on his face.

Five minutes later, Mac stood outside the watertight door separating the engineering spaces from the more habitable crew spaces. The door served two purposes. In the event of a fire, it would keep heat and smoke out of the rest of the ship. It would also isolate the engineering spaces in the event of flooding. The door was steel and very sturdy. In this case, the ship's engineers had welded the latches shut from the inside to keep the pirates out.

Mac grabbed a demolition axe from a holder on the wall and struck the door three times. A few minutes later, two strikes came from inside. Mac hit the door one more time, and a small portal opened.

"What's the password, Mac?" a voice on the inside asked.

"Clive Cussler."

"Roger that, sir, give us ten minutes to cut the welds and we'll open her up."

"Okay. The Navy's taken our ship back. Get everyone working as soon as you can."

"Will do."

As Mac headed back toward the bridge, the SEAL team leader tapped him on the shoulder and motioned for him to wait. The SEAL was listening to a radio call in his earpiece.

"Copy that, I'll tell him." Turning to Mac, he spoke. "Blackie's conscious. My medic says Black needs to talk to you ASAP."

Mac nodded and headed toward his cabin at a fast walk.

Chapter 29

Mac's cabin was crowded. Cat was offered the only chair, leaving Mac, the SEAL team leader, and one medic standing. It felt like they were all crowded in the same telephone booth to Mac. "How are you, John?"

"That's unimportant right now. Cat says they have two bombs on the surface; is that correct?" John Black looked slightly better. He lay in Mac's bunk with an IV in one arm and a bag of blood product rigged into his other arm.

"We think so. Let's assume the answer is yes."

"Then you need to get underway and put as much space between *Atlantis* and the weapons. They may go off."

"What? How? The bombs are thirty years old!"

"Mac, my old friend, I'll explain later. Get her underway then come back and see me for your lesson in thermonuclear weapons. Right now, I'm tired. Get your ass moving, and I'll take a nap."

Mac scowled. "Very well, John." He turned and picked up his phone that went directly to the bridge. "Make preparations to get underway immediately, flank speed. I don't care. Tell him the bus is leaving."

Cat reached for Mac's arm, "Sir, Homer is still deployed on the bottom."

"I'm sorry, Miss King. We'll come back for him. Call the riggers and tell them to cut the cables. He's done his job on this mission." Mac stood and headed for the bridge. As he walked, he could hear the main engines starting up.

He walked onto the bridge and folded his lanky frame into his place in his chair. Turning to the helmsman, he asked, "How long?"

"Engineer says we can be underway in two minutes, sir. What course?"

Pointing out the port windows toward the brightly lit salvage vessel, he said, "Away from that." He glanced around his bridge. The crew had made an effort to clean the decks of the blood and brains of the terrorists, but there was still material on the walls. The bodies were gone, apparently bagged and removed by the SEAL team. The bridge windows still had small holes with spider cracks around them.

Cat and the SEAL team leader entered the bridge, Cat holding a mug of coffee for Mac.

"Thanks for the coffee. Did the riggers get the cables cut? I'd hate to drag him away from your coordinates."

"Yes, they got the cables cut but not until we dragged him about a mile. I'll have to look at the ship's plotter and try to back into a location. I hope we can find him."

"Captain MacAdams." The SEAL team leader spoke up. "In case you were wondering, my men have Michael and his friends, both the live ones and the ones on their way to meet Allah, under guard in your spare parts conex."

Mac spun his chair to better face the young man. "Thank you, I had thought about where they were, but I guess I just assumed you had that under control. By the way, I have to apologize. I haven't even taken the time to thank you and your team. What's your name, young man?"

"Ragan, sir. Lieutenant Ragan. The Navy is glad to have been able to assist."

Mac extended his hand, and the two shook. "Thank you, Lieutenant, thank you for helping John as well. What do your medics say?"

Ragan shook his head. "Hard to say. My guys are among the best. Actually all the special ops medical specialists can perform miracles. Problem is their skillset, equipment, and drugs are designed to stabilize someone and keep them alive for an hour or so until they can be heloed to a forward area medical unit. Blackie's stable, but they can't go in and get the bullet or patch up what's causing the internal bleeding."

Cat seemed to visibly deflate. "So there's nothing that can be done?"

"I don't think so, but you never know."

"What if we head for Greenland?" Mac asked. "In twelve hours or so we could be in range of a helicopter to take him to a real hospital."

"I'll ask. I don't know if they considered that, but it's certainly worth trying."

A SEAL stuck his head in the door. "Blackie would like to see you. He said it was time for your lesson."

The three stood and headed across the hallway to Mac's room, now occupied by John Black and one of the medics. They gave the seat to Cat; the others stood.

Mac was actually quite surprised to see the difference in John's appearance. His color was improved. Hell, just being conscious was amazing. His eyes were somewhat glazed, likely a reaction to the morphine. "Okay, we're here. Is this going to be our lesson in nuclear physics?"

A wry smile appeared on the patient's face. "No, physics is way over your heads, with the possible exception of King here." He pointed weakly at Cat. "How far are we from the bombs right now?"

"About five miles is my guess."

"Okay, we're safe from the first possibility. Don't slow down until you have twenty-five miles of separation."

"How can there be a danger from a bomb that's been on the bottom for thirty years?" Mac asked.

"I can see how you would think that. The batteries have to be dead, right?"

"Exactly." Mac nodded.

"Okay, thermonuclear bomb lesson number one. A hydrogen bomb needs two fission bombs to detonate simultaneously with a hydrogen source between them. The two fission bombs provide the heat and pressure to cause hydrogen to fuse into helium with a huge release of energy. The odds of those bombs producing a fusion detonation are pretty much zero."

"That's good to know."

"Agreed, my friend. That leaves us with the fission bombs. They're essentially a sphere of plutonium surrounded by plastic explosive segments shaped to implode the plutonium to a core that will result in a runaway nuclear reaction called an atomic bomb. The technology really hasn't changed a lot since Hiroshima."

"Got that. Continue, professor."

"There are numerous safeties, but let's assume the crew wasn't able to put the weapons in a totally safe condition. If they had, hell, you could crash a B-52 loaded with weapons onboard and it could burn to a crisp on the runway with no danger of detonating."

"That's happened, hasn't it?" Cat asked.

"Absolutely, a few times. In a fire, the plutonium is a problem, toxic as hell, but the explosives, no big deal. They just burn like Sterno. We can agree the batteries are dead. The problem is the detonators. There are about a hundred of them, and electronically, they're like a capacitor, so they can store power more or less forever. The problem is they've been in salt water. No telling where corrosion has created a potential short."

"And that's the problem?" Mac asked quietly.

John closed his eyes and grimaced quietly.

Mac turned to Ragan. "Can we get him something for pain?"

Ragan nodded.

"No!" John exclaimed. "Let me finish, and then I'll take my morphine. You need to get with the ragheads and tell them there's an excellent chance the weapons could go off with at least a detonation of the plastic explosives. As a minimum, it would blow a ship to hell and scatter plutonium all over the place. Or worse."

"So, what do you recommend, other than putting miles between us and them?"

"Probably a waste of time, but see if you can convince them they're in mortal danger. The weapons need to be in a bath of distilled water, or at least fresh water. If they know how, all the detonators need to be disconnected. Which will be trickier than shit."

Mac turned to Ragan. "Can you have your translator give it a try?"

He nodded. "What are you guys' thoughts on my explaining this to Michael and letting him try to persuade them?"

"Fine with me, but I'd have your translator there. If they want to be asses about it, it's their funeral."

Cat blurted out, "Don't be confused. I'll not shed a tear over them, but a detonation like that will leave a possible plutonium cloud drifting who knows where."

"I see your point, but all we can do is warn them, isn't it? That and pray Blackie's wrong. Life sucks, doesn't it?"

"No shit, Mac."

Chapter 30

Onboard Atlantis

Mac and Ragan headed back to the bridge. Cat and the medic stayed with John. As soon as they stepped over the sill onto the bridge, a SEAL approached Ragan. He nodded and stepped outside to the bridge wing and pulled a portable radio from one of the pockets in his vest.

MacAdams took his place in his chair and looked out the bridge windows as the sun climbed slowly into the sky. Back home it was the end of summer. Trees would begin to show some colors in a few weeks, and in a month, there could be frost early in the morning.

At this latitude, daybreak was later than back in Massachusetts, and the sun was at a much lower angle in the sky. The nearly calm seas that had existed for the previous twelve hours or so had changed to a moderate chop, and gray clouds and a breeze out of the north seemed to signal the days of summer were definitely gone on the North Atlantic for this year.

Mac's stomach told him it was time for breakfast. As he began to mull over the possibilities with some appeal, Ragan stepped back onto the bridge. "A moment, Captain?"

Mac nodded, stood, and headed for the wardroom. Filling another cup as he entered the room, he realized he had been running exclusively on coffee for about thirty-six hours now. He needed a meal and sleep, desperately. "What's up, Lieutenant?"

"I have new instructions from *Alabama*, sir. Captain is going to want you to stop soon, no need to tell you where or when, and *Alabama*'s going to surface ahead of us. I'm to send most of my men and gear back aboard *Alabama*. I'll stay, along with a few men. My captain tells me the Iranian sub has slinked away. He says the Navy wants him to tail them and be prepared to take action when ordered."

"What sort of action?"

"Not determined yet. Also, there is a surface ship close to arriving. It's a Navy frigate. They've been on the way from off New York. It was just a matter of *Alabama* being the closest thing with a SEAL team aboard."

"I wondered about why we hadn't seen a surface ship…"

"Yeah, I can see that. Anyway, they should be on station in another six hours. So, *Alabama* is leaving us as soon as she picks up my guys."

"Thanks for the information, Lieutenant."

"Yes, sir. Now I'm headed to the ragheads, sorry, pirates, to see if we can get Michael to put the fear of Allah into the guys on the ship about the weapons. Maybe they can get up with the sub."

Onboard Alabama

"Captain's on the bridge."

The announcement rang out in the control room aboard *Alabama*. Commander Johnson had made sure Ragan's SEAL team members were safely aboard and everything was stowed, hatches locked and sealed, and the sub was ready to submerge. It wasn't necessary for the sub's captain to do this personally. It was simply a matter of Johnson liking to look the guys in the eyes and ask them how the mission had gone. From what he saw and heard, all had gone well.

Turning to the officer of the deck, he said, in a rather calm tone, "Go ahead and take her down."

The officer of the deck got on the PA. "Dive, dive, dive." Diving in a modern sub was far different from the frantic action portrayed in WWII movies. *Alabama* wasn't under attack; there was no rush. Nowadays it was simply a matter of placing slight positive pressure in the boat to assure there were no open hatches or vents, verifying all the crew was inside, and opening the vents in the external tanks that held enough air to temporarily turn the sub into a surface vessel.

At that point *Alabama* would quietly slip below the surface and return to her normal state, a steel fish in its natural habitat.

Johnson turned to the Combat Information Center officer. "Range and bearing to the sub."

"Six miles, zero-six-zero, sir."

"Depth?"

"Three hundred feet, sir."

"Very well." Turning to the officer of the deck, he spoke. "Make fifteen knots. Close to two miles behind them and then match their speed. Hold a depth of one hundred fifty feet."

"Sir? Awfully shallow."

"I know. Ragan says there's a chance the bombs could potentially detonate. I don't want to be too close. Being shallow lessens a shock wave to us if that were to happen."

"Understood, sir." With that, the officer of the deck issued orders to the men manning the propulsion, depth, and heading controls.

"Now we simply tail them and wait for further instructions," Captain Johnson said quietly. *Or a loud bang.*

Onboard Atlantis
1100 hrs

Cat walked into the wardroom, searching for Mac. She found him sleeping on the red leather couch. His body was too long for it, and he looked miserable to her. She decided not to disturb him. The smell of stale coffee interrupted her exit. As she poured a mug, she realized she needed sleep a lot worse than caffeine. Holding her mug, she turned and headed for the door.

"Don't go. How long have I been out?"

"I'm not sure. I haven't seen you in a couple hours."

"Have you slept?"

"I guess," she lied. "I think I caught some micro-naps in the chair in your cabin."

"How's John?"

"I'm not sure how to answer. The medic says technically he should be dying, but he looks better. His vitals are better than they were, and when he's lucid, as in just before they give him morphine, he's quite rational. Just from what I can see, they aren't having to give him as much blood."

"Seen Ragan lately?"

"No."

Mac stood, slowly and painfully. His normally painful joints had not been helped any by his nap. "Let's go find him. I need to see how the conversation went with Michael's friends."

The two walked out to the bridge. Mac asked the helmsman how things were going.

"Just fine, sir."

"Good, can you please find Lieutenant Ragan?"

"Will do, sir." The young man got on his portable radio and put out a page for the lieutenant.

Mac could hear Ragan's reply on the portable radio that he would be up to the bridge in five minutes. With that, Mac took his place in his chair. *Should've grabbed a nap here. At least it's more comfortable than that damned couch.* Turning to Cat, he spoke quietly, "You should get some sleep, Miss King."

"You should follow your own advice, sir," she replied with a tired version of a grin.

The two conveyed their individual exhaustion silently with their facial expressions. Cat placed her hand over Mac's to cement her suggestion.

Ragan appeared on the bridge wearing clean, dry clothing. He was still in "ready for action" clothing. Pants with multiple pockets full of God knew what, a ballistic vest with more pockets, and a camo shirt. His clothing and his Salomon Quest boots looked like they had seen months of use in places the United States government would deny he had been to.

"Good morning, Lieutenant. I'm glad to see you in dry clothes. How did that happen?"

Ragan grinned. "When *Alabama* picked up the rest of my guys, they sent us more duds. That and a shower can work wonders. By the way, Captain, you and Miss King look like you could both use some sleep."

"Thanks for your concern. As I'm sure you can understand, command brings responsibilities with it. I'm not quite to a point I feel comfortable clocking out."

"Nor do I, even though there isn't much I'm in command of," Cat echoed.

"At any rate, how did the conversation go with our opposition?"

"Not well, sir. I actually think Michael understood the issue and did his best to persuade them they needed to take action. His, and their, motives are in opposition to ours, but the bottom line is I don't think he wants his guys to die. I think he believed us."

"But?"

"But they basically told us to pound sand. My translator listened closely. He says Michael made an honest effort. Over and above what my guy said was probably realistic for us to expect. By the way, they told us both weapons are on the sub and have left the area. As we discussed, *Alabama* is tailing them. At this point, that's it."

"Is there a reason you and the rest of your squad are still with us?"

"Aside from the fact that you have better groceries, and a few women, our commanders apparently think there might still be a threat to you guys."

"Well, I hope that they're wrong, but I'm personally happy to have your protection. You're welcome to our food, such as it is. We need to re-provision. Now, as far as our women..." Mac grinned and hit Ragan in the arm. "That is an altogether different matter. Have we managed to find your men a place to sleep?"

"Yes, sir, your engineer made some arrangements. We're good."

Mac turned to his helmsman. "Distance to the salvage ship?"

"Thirty-five miles sir. They're headed away and speeding up."

Turning to Ragan, he asked, "What do you think they're up to?"

"I think they have decided to run as a convoy. They can protect each other if the surface ship has offensive weapons."

"Weapons? What sort?"

"Ship-to-ship missiles, ground-to-air, stuff like that. I don't have any inside information, but it would make sense."

"Yes, it does. The other weapons, the nukes, are out of our hands then, I suppose. What are your thoughts? What do you think the Navy's plans are for the sub?"

"At this point I don't know. I can tell you this. Before my crew left *Alabama*, my understanding from my C.O. was that the weapons weren't going to get away."

"Meaning whatever it took?"

Ragan nodded silently.

"Good." It was Cat speaking.

Chapter 31

Mac, Cat, and Ragan sat in the wardroom quietly eating TV dinners. Bread was long stale and thrown overboard, fresh vegetables nonexistent. *Atlantis* needed fuel and replenishment. Under normal circumstances, Mac would have slowed *Atlantis* down from the headlong rush she was in.

Initially the speed had been for separation from the bombs. Now Mac was hoping to get close enough to Greenland for a helicopter to pick John Black up for movement to a hospital.

"Are you sure the Navy frigate can't help John in their sick bay?" he asked Ragan between bites.

"Pretty sure. Honestly my guys are better. Any serious injury on a vessel like a frigate will be airlifted to a carrier or cruiser, something with an operating room and a doctor. I *will* have my guys resupply on some meds for him. We're running low."

"When do you think we'll be seeing the frigate?"

Ragan looked at his watch. "We should be hearing from them on the VHF within the hour. My guess is we'll be looking at them in a few hours."

"Good. I sent an email back to Woods Hole as soon as I got up via the satellite link requesting a helo to extract John. They'll be checking to see what's available and their range. I should hear back from them pretty soon."

"That would be a relief," Cat sighed. "John and the medics insist he's terminal, no hope. I refuse to accept that."

"And well you should. You assholes aren't getting rid of me that easily."

Mac spun around. John Fucking Black was standing in the doorway with a sheepish grin on his face and an exasperated looking medical tech behind him.

"I want you guys to know I'm damned sick and tired of this motley crew making all these decisions without my astute advice!"

"John, what in the hell are you doing out of bed?" Cat jumped up and navigated around the table to hug him. "Here, sit down. Again, what the hell…?"

He gingerly took a seat. He extended a hand to Ragan. "John Fucking Black. Nice to meet you. And you are?"

"Lieutenant Ragan, SEAL Team leader, *USS Alabama*, Mr. Black. It's not often I get to meet a legend. You are quite well known in our little community."

"I suppose that would be true. You should consider the probability that much of the good *and* bad you might have heard are probably vastly exaggerated."

Ragan smiled. "I'll keep that in mind, Blackie."

During all this, Mac had quietly stood, gone to a cabinet, and poured a very small shot of Stoli. He handed it to his old friend. "I'm positive this is not permitted." He was looking at the medical tech as he delivered the drink. "But if you're going to die anyway, what could it hurt?"

The medical tech shrugged and rolled his eyes.

"Seriously, John, what's going on? Don't lie to me either. I'll just get this young man to tell me the truth," Mac challenged.

"First, I refuse to sample this unexpected gift alone. Unless all of you join me in a toast to Ragan and his team, I'll pour it in the sink."

"I think he's serious," Cat said, smiling. She gathered more glasses and passed them out. The bottle of vodka went around the room, and everyone held their glasses up, looking at John expectantly.

He raised his glass. "To the SEALs." And he tossed the half-ounce or so down. The others followed suit. "As I was saying, second, with regard to my medical condition, my doctor has been simply amazed. I appear to have clotted internally to the point that I'm now simply leaking like an old, wooden boat. No longer gushing like the *Titanic*." He turned to the tech. "Have I lied?"

"You haven't lied, sir. On the other hand, you haven't told the whole truth either."

"Well, you tell them the rest. It's all B.S. anyway in my humble opinion."

The medical tech sighed. "Okay, from my experience, my patient should be dead. As we can all see, apparently my experience is wrong. The only possible reason he isn't is that the bullet was a small caliber and must have danced around some. That's assuming we exclude divine intervention., which seems pretty obvious to me. I can almost guarantee Mr. Black has kidney and liver damage. It should have damaged his spleen, but he tells me that's been removed. Bottom line, by now the S.O.B. should be dead. Obviously, he isn't. I can tell you if he does something to break the clots he seems to have formed, he could bleed out in a short period of time."

Mac looked at the tech. "Has Blackie been a good patient?"

"Are you serious? Hell no. On the other hand, SEALs always suck as patients anyway. They seem to have an invulnerability complex. I've had a couple tell me they were good to go just before they died, so I can't say Black is a total surprise."

Mac turned to John Black. "Blackie, do us all a favor. Go back to bed."

"I will, as soon as I've been updated to our current situation."

Mac sighed. "Okay. Lt. Ragan, will you please update John?"

Ragan smiled and presented a *Reader's Digest* version of what had occurred since he came aboard.

"So, the bombs are on the sub?" John asked.

"That's what we understand right now."

"And you've warned them about the chances the shit could hit the fan?"

"Absolutely. They more or less told us to shove it."

Black seemed to be thinking before he replied. "Okay. On the one hand, it would be a blessing to western civilization if it turned out I was right and the sub blew to hell. On the other hand, is there a plan to keep the ragheads from delivering the plutonium to people that will use it on us?"

"There is." Ragan replied. "I don't know what the plan is, but when I last spoke to the captain of *Alabama*, he indicated his orders were to prevent that. Whatever it took."

"Thank God. Maybe the bastards that run things in D.C. have acquired some realistic attitudes. That would be a welcome change."

"No disagreement here," Mac said quietly as he returned to his seat.

An *Atlantis* bridge crewmember stuck his head in the door, papers in hand. "Sorry to interrupt, but we just received an urgent email for you sir." He spoke in a low tone of voice as he handed the papers to Mac.

Mac pulled his reading glasses from his pocket and read the message. When he finished, he turned to Ragan. "Granted, it *is* the United States Navy, but I must say your people are pretty skilled in the information-collection business, Lieutenant. The email is intended for both of us, but given the present company, I'll read it aloud. Would someone please secure the door?"

To: M.J. MacAdams, Master, Vessel Atlantis/*Lt. C.C. Ragan, SEAL Team Commander*

From: Lt. Commander P.L. Sullivan, Commander, USS Reuben James

Gentlemen – Our understanding is Atlantis *has no method of secure communications, and we are still out of range of Ragan's tactical radio. We estimate being on station in 2 hrs. Be advised* Alabama *reports an explosive detonation aboard sub under surveillance and subsequent sinking of same. Cause of detonation unknown, but* Alabama *reports this was not, repeat not, a discharge of a nuclear nature.* Alabama *advises increase of radioactive level in the water. She also advises indication of increased levels of activity aboard salvage vessel. CNO has been notified and instructed we notify you.*

Sullivan/End of message

"It would appear you were right to be concerned, John," Cat said. "We can only hope both weapons were onboard the sub. If they went off, they would they scatter plutonium into the water, right?"

A grunt of agreement took place around the table. Mac easily felt the collective sigh of relief, and he suspected the others seated at the table felt it as well.

His slightly relaxed attitude was short-lived. A knock on the wardroom door interrupted his sense of relief. "Come."

"Captain, you're needed on the bridge."

"What's up?"

"*Salvage One* is hailing us on the VHF, declaring an emergency."

"Very well. Get the engineer up here as well, ASAP."

The young man nodded and left the room.

"Well, Mac, we all knew it was too good to last." Blackie put a period on MacAdams' thoughts.

"Right as usual, my friend, right as usual." He rose from his chair and headed for the bridge.

Chapter 32

On the Bridge

"Master *Atlantis*, this is Master *Savage One* requesting assistance, over."

Mac walked to the console, picked up the microphone to the VHF radio, and then replaced it in its holder. He stepped back and took his seat. He decided he would wait for his engineer. Meanwhile, Cat and Ragan had stepped onto the bridge, which was now becoming slightly crowded.

Salvage One called two more times before Mac's chief engineer had time to make his way to the bridge. The faceless voice on the other end of the radio had a definite sound of panic.

"How can I help, sir?" the engineer asked, slightly breathless from a rapid trip up three decks.

"The pirate ship is asking for assistance. I haven't answered yet. I wanted you to hear what they're asking for so I can tell them what we can or can't do for them."

"Why don't we simply tell them to eat shit and die? Just my opinion, sir. No offense."

Mac sighed. "None taken. However, a ship's captain is ultimately responsible for the lives of his crew. I can appreciate that regardless of anything else that may have happened."

"Too sympathetic, Mac," Cat interjected.

"Maybe, but he's got a point." Ragan threw his two cents worth in.

"Master *Atlantis*, this is Master *Salvage One*. Come in *Atlantis*. We have an emergency, and you are closest vessel, over."

Mac stood and walked to the radio. "This is *Atlantis*. What is the nature of your emergency?" He turned to look at the radar. *Salvage One* was visible on the screen at a range of about seventy miles.

"We are taking on water and our engines have been damaged, rendering our pumps inoperative."

"So, you need pumps?"

"Affirmative."

"May I ask what happened?"

"As you probably know, our companion had an explosion while running close by."

Mac paused for a moment, considering his words. "I hope you realize we were not responsible."

"We accept you at your word. There is something else."

"Go ahead..."

"I am violating orders, but I am concerned for my crew. Your people tried to convince us the weapons could be a danger. It would seem that may have caused the problem with the sub."

"Yes, it could have. You should have heeded our advice."

"Yes, you are right. The problem is that one of the weapons is still on my ship."

Mac felt a chill come over him. "What are you asking of me? Jettison it over the side. Save yourselves. Do it now."

"My men, they are frightened, they will not come near it. They see the bomb as possessed. We believe you have someone on board that could make it safe. I beg you, by all that is holy. Please, save my ship, save my crew."

"Don't do it, Mac." It was John Black. He had eased onto the bridge. "Don't go within ten, no, twenty miles of them."

Mac realized he could be right. "You must realize I can't come anywhere near your vessel without threatening my own ship."

Silence.

"I have an idea. We have a large launch. It will hold quite a few people. I can send it toward you. Give me coordinates and I will send them. Please, help me save my crew."

Ragan shook his head.

Mac began to think over his options. "Give me time to consider this. I'll call you back. Out." He turned around. "John, Ragan, Cat, wardroom, now." Looking over his shoulder, he said to the helmsman, "Set a course for them, and hurry."

In the wardroom

Cat looked at MacAdams as she poured a mug of coffee that was several hours past its prime. "You aren't seriously considering helping them, are you?"

Mac was the last one to enter the wardroom. He shut the door and grabbed a mug of the brown battery acid. He took his seat at the head of the table. There were several conversations ongoing; at least it seemed that way. He respected his crew but realized, as the captain, he was the ultimate and final authority. The chatter eventually died down, and everyone began to stare at him.

"My mind is made up. We are going to do what we can to help. Lt. Ragan, I'm assuming the *Reuben James* has a helo?"

"Yes, sir, they do."

"Then I need you to find a way to contact them and ask how many people they can pick up here and move to *Salvage One*. Until the bomb is safed, whatever that requires, I won't put anyone aboard to help with regards to pumps or any other mechanical assistance. John, I hate to ask, because I realize I'm risking your life, but do you see any chance of eliminating a possibility of detonation?"

"Mac, you must be kidding. The man is doing good to stand upright!" Cat exclaimed.

"Of course, you're right. But—"

"I'll do it, Mac. But I need Cat too."

Mac was taken aback. "Cat? Are you shitting me? Why?"

John Black looked at Cat then turned to Mac. "It's like this, my old friend. I'm weak and old. Her hands are smaller, and she's got amazing abilities with wiring, and..." He looked toward Cat with what Mac saw as a pleading face.

Cat took the hint. "Mac, we probably should have mentioned it, but John and I have worked together before. In similar situations. John is brilliant, amazing actually, but I'm pretty good at this too. Given his present condition, I think he's right."

"Should have mentioned it before? Ya think? Jesus Christ on a skateboard, I knew you were a spook, but you *and* John? Holy shit!"

Cat looked at John, and he nodded. "John and I have done something similar, twice. Once when the Israelis lost one just offshore in the Med. We located it and safed it for them. The other time was more complicated. The Russians lost a nuclear-tipped torpedo in the Black Sea. A fisherman brought it up in his net. He was smart enough to know what he had and wanted to sell it on the black market. The Agency found out about it. John's SEAL team got involved. It was kinda hairy. Bad deal that turned out well, I suppose."

"Except that it cost me my career with the Navy, but Cat was amazing, top of the line. She sees the wiring in her mind. I need her on this, Mac, if you expect this to go well."

"My better judgement says hell no, but if the two of you are telling me that's what needs to happen, what else can I say? Very well. Ragan, what do we need to do for you to be able to talk to *Reuben James*?"

"Sir, I'm thinking maybe if I get up on the mast, I may be able to talk to them with my tactical radio. I'll try now."

"Okay, because there's no way I'm sending John and Cat to an enemy ship without an armed escort. I'm assuming you would be willing and able to send an escort with them?"

"Absolutely, sir. I agree. That's why my squad and I are still here."

"Okay. If I have my way, *Reuben James* will send a helo. Your med tech will give John whatever drugs he needs to keep him alive, and we ship them and at least two SEALs with them. I think these guys are desperate, but I don't trust them any further than I can throw them."

"Thank you, Mac," Cat said, putting her arm around him. "We are the best people to try to accomplish this. I know this is a difficult decision, but you're doing the most intelligent thing that can be done under the circumstances, with the possible exception of running like hell."

Mac almost grinned. "I hope you're right because I have a very bad feeling about this."

Chapter 33

The helo was crowded. Weight wasn't a problem; the Sikorsky UH-60 helicopter was designed to carry two anti-sub torpedoes. Offloading these had created a huge additional carrying capacity from a weight standpoint. The problem was that the aircraft was designed to carry a crew of two to four passengers due to the specialized anti-sub equipment. There were seven onboard, as well as equipment John and Cat had decided to bring.

It had been a somewhat harrowing flight. Once Ragan had contacted the Navy frigate by hanging off the mast of *Atlantis*, the flight had been planned and prepared. The helo had hovered over *Atlantis*'s deck and winched up the passengers one at a time as *Atlantis* cruised at about five knots into the wind. All this in total darkness.

After loading up John, Cat, and their three-SEAL escort, the chopper turned and headed toward *Salvage One*. As the chopper skimmed over the cold, dark seas, John Black leaned toward Cat. Cupping his hand to her ear, he spoke as quietly as the noise level in the aircraft permitted. "Do you feel like we told Mac a whopper?"

She looked down, thinking. "Yes and no. We probably could have been more honest up front about having worked together in the past. If we lied, I suppose it was by omission."

"I guess. The only thing I ask myself is, would we, or Mac, have done anything differently? That's really the bottom line, but we'll never know the answer."

Ragan leaned forward, motioning for John and Cat to put on their headsets. He spoke into the intercom. "I've decided when we get there, my team and I exit first. I want these guys to understand any attempt to do anything other than cooperate with you two won't be tolerated. As a minimum, I presume you want them to stay out of your way."

John nodded. "If it's as their commander indicated, I'm expecting the crew is going to stay as far away from the weapon, and us, as possible."

"Do you really think they might try anything?" Cat asked.

"Don't think so," Ragan replied, shaking his head. "But you never know if one of them might want to collect his seventy-two virgins in the afterlife. Let's just hope not."

The helicopter pilot's voice came over the headsets. "We've got the ship on radar. It's about six miles out. We should be able to see her by now. She's totally dark."

Ragan spoke. "Our understanding is the ship has no power, no propulsion either."

"Copy that. I can light it up with our own lights. It'll be a little tough, but nothing like landing on *Reuben James* in high seas at night. When we arrive, I'll circle a few times to check it out." Everyone in the rear compartment heard a click indicating the pilot had switched over to speak to his copilot, cutting him off from the passengers.

A few minutes later, the UH-60 began to slowly orbit the salvage ship. It was John and Cat's first close look at the ship that had been their nemesis for the last thirty-six hours or so. The ship was large; it looked to be nearly three hundred feet in length. The aft equipment area was twice the size of *Atlantis*'s work zone. This ship also had a dedicated helicopter pad. The ship was impressive and crippled. *Salvage One* rolled lightly in the low swells. She was totally dark.

As they peered out the window on the chopper, the helicopter landing pad suddenly lit up. John got on the intercom. "Looks like they're using a portable generator."

Ragan nodded. "Someone realizes it would be a touchy job to land in total darkness. My guess is our pilots will appreciate it."

Moments later, the helo was on the deck. Ragan and his men exited first. They formed an armed perimeter, securing the area. Ragan found a man in uniform that approached him. The two spoke briefly, and Ragan returned to the helicopter. "You two can get out. I'll help you with your equipment. I told their captain if he wants to disarm the devil on the stern he needs to get some people to rig some lights. Follow me."

Ragan escorted John and Cat off the helipad. As soon as the group cleared the area, the helicopter lifted off and headed back toward the *Reuben James*.

"While we were enroute, the pilot told me the Navy ship is coming here. They will be seizing *Salvage One*, and the bomb of course. The ship's crew will be charged with piracy, assuming the ship doesn't sink."

"Or blow up," John said quietly.

The group made their way down several flights of stairs of superstructure to the aft equipment deck. A few members of the crew were in a group rigging up a portable light stand and carrying a small generator. Moments later the generator roared to life, and the scene was lit up. The star of the show was a long cylindrical object covered by a tarpaulin. They all realized the innocuous-looking tarp covered a thirty-year-old weapon of mass destruction. A city killer.

In a strange, ironic twist, that weapon, and thousands of others like it, had turned out to be weapons of peace. Only the threat of mutually assured destruction had kept the world's superpowers from destroying each other.

"Time to go to work, Cat," John said quietly. The two pulled the tarp back to expose the pitted, discolored aluminum cylinder. "A WA-52," he commented in a remarkably calm voice.

She nodded, opening one of the tool kits. "So, what's the plan?"

"Really no accepted protocol for this. My guess would be we disconnect the batteries then discharge all the capacitors. Your thoughts?"

"Agreed, I'd say we clip all the wires from the plastic pack detonators after that. You do realize we'll be exposed to the plutonium core without any lead gloves and shielding when we do that, right?"

"Wrong. I'll be exposed, not you."

"But, John, my hands are smaller. I can get to them easier."

"You're right of course, but there's something you haven't considered. I'm dying."

"No, they say you're holding your own. We're going to get you in helicopter range very soon. We can—"

"No, you don't understand. If I had never taken a bullet, I'm still dying. Pancreatic cancer. A month, maybe two, and I'll be bedridden and taking pain shots, probably smoking pot, heroin, hell, anything and everything. Because it won't really matter."

"Shit, John! How the fuck can you have kept something like that from me? From Mac?" She started beating him about his shoulders, tears beginning to stream down her face. "It's just so fucking wrong…"

John Black put his arms around her. "What you see as selfish is, well, you're wrong. Had this gig not come up, I would have self-medicated with enough Stoli to float a small boat. Mac would have been forced to suspend me, and I would have disappeared somewhere. A few months later, I'd be in a flag-draped coffin with a very small number of people crying and a much larger group smiling and saying good riddance."

She put her head on his shoulder for a few moments then backed away and wiped her tears. "All right then. Since you have all this worked out, we should get to work, you fucking asshole." A small, forced smile began to appear on her face.

"One more thing. There are two envelopes with my gear on *Atlantis*, one for you, one for Mac. Be sure you two read them. Some of it's important. Of course, some of it's bullshit. You're right. Let's go to work."

He motioned toward the weapon. "Help me get the access panels off. We can set up the ground straps, lay out the tools, and then you need to get over there"—he pointed toward a large crane base—"and stay away from the hot zone until I can put the covers back on."

"Yes, boss. I'll do it. You're still an ass though."

"We all know that."

Chapter 34

Onboard Salvage One
One hour later

Cat watched John as he tinkered in the guts of the weapon. She wanted to be taking part in the action, knowing she could have helped. John worked slowly, methodically, a miner's light strapped to his head illuminating the immediate work area. The batteries had come out first, and then the real work had begun. She knew from personal experience it would have been much better to have had access to a schematic wiring diagram.

On the other hand, since weapons of this type had been around for fifty years now, the wiring was nearly identical. Weapons that went on top of missiles were an entirely different story. The same work on one of those would take much longer, and entirely different equipment.

Ragan had walked over a few times, once just to chat, the other time to tell her *Reuben James* was just over the horizon, maybe three or four miles across the black, cold sea. The two would smoke as they watched Blackie from a safe distance.

Reuben James had slowly slid aside while John worked. Cat turned to Ragan. "Do they realize how important it is that John's not disturbed?"

"Yes, I didn't tell them exactly why, only that the situation involved a bomb being defused. They intend to put people and pumps aboard, but not back here."

"And the crew?"

"I don't think they have that exactly figured out. If they can prevent the ship from sinking, they'll probably put it in tow and place it and its crew in custody somewhere. Above my pay grade."

"Mine as well." She turned back to watch John as he worked. Her mind drifted back to the first time the two of them had worked together.

Three years earlier

As the op began, she hadn't realized or been told John and the specialized SEAL team would be involved.

In hindsight, she should have anticipated it. A call had come from out of the blue. Her CIA handler had instructions. One moment she was sitting in her cube as a civilian DOD employee, and eighteen hours later she was in Romania. Her handlers had decided to send her in to examine a Russian torpedo.

She and a CIA agent were to act as potential buyers of the weapon. The agent was supposed to be the "money guy," and Cat was there as a tech nerd to verify that the torpedo was indeed a nuclear-tipped weapon.

There were multiple potential buyers, at least four different languages, and every potential buyer seemed to have a gun and a small army of bodyguards. Except for Cat and the idiot the Agency had sent her in with.

It hadn't begun that badly, at least it had seemed okay until she actually met her "partner," Tim. He seemed to see himself as a James Bond wannabe. As Cat had understood the briefing, the CIA's analysts had recommended being vague about who Cat and her partner were representing. Instead her partner had seemed to think it would be a smart move to represent the two of them as working for an unnamed Arab entity.

The "sellers" of the weapon were Romanians. They seemed to have been trained by the KGB and appeared to be pretty smart. The problem was that there *were* actually Arab bidders. Cat realized she was a techno geek. Actually being involved in the "deal" was above her pay grade and outside her experience level with the Agency, but she had quickly realized her partner as a disaster waiting to happen.

The sellers had allowed all of the bidders to examine the device prior to the start of the bidding. This was her area of expertise, and she was ready and experienced in that aspect. She and her partner were given directions to a warehouse several miles outside of Constanta, after the sellers had confiscated their cellphones and searched them. She and Tim had argued during the entire trip. He seemed to have absolutely no use for any input on her part.

Upon arrival at their destination, they were escorted by the sellers into a warehouse near the port.

This part of the assignment was Cat's specialty. They were guided into a part of a larger building curtained off from the rest. Cat had toolboxes of items to help her verify that they were looking at a Soviet torpedo with a nuclear warhead. Tim carried a small suitcase full of cash.

Eventually they were taken into the area cordoned off by curtains. Tim helped carry her toolboxes, but once they were actually looking at the weapon, he set the cases down and began bullshitting with their escorts.

Cat slowly walked around the torpedo. It was about eight meters long and about a half-meter in diameter. That corresponded to what should have been the physical dimensions of a Russian torpedo. The Cyrillic labelling on the exterior of the fish was correct, including the symbols indicating that the warhead was nuclear. But all that was simply paint. Cat was there for a reason. Her job was to verify this was a nuke. It would take more than paint to convince her of that fact.

The next step would be to use a Gieger-Meuller probe to detect radioactivity. While most investigators would stop there, Cat had already decided that was not going to be conclusive in her examination. Any sophisticated entity trying to sell a bill of goods could simply insert some fissionable material inside a metal warhead shell attempting to deceive a sucker to pay huge dollars for a fake.

Cat knew the steps needed to examine the interior of a warhead to know a nuke from a fake. It was the only reason she was here. She knew it, "Tim" knew it, and the Romanians were about to realize it. She turned to the second toolbox and began to remove the access plates on the warhead.

Fifteen minutes later she was done. After examining the normal triggers that would be on a torpedo, regardless of whether it held a conventional or nuclear warhead, she followed the firing circuit back to a stainless bulkhead. Way too many wires penetrated the bulkhead. Plastic explosive would have needed only a single set of wires for detonation. She turned to Tim and nodded. "It's the real thing." Now it was all on him.

He had told her the Romanians had tough conditions. Each bidder had been required to deliver fifty thousand dollars U.S. in cash as a good faith deposit. Said deposit was naturally non-refundable. The successful high bidder would then have to make a wire transfer to a bank in Zurich. Then, and only then, would the weapon change hands. Tim made a big show of placing the suitcase on a table and opening the combination locks. He opened the case and slid it to the Romanians. Everyone smiled, except Cat.

They were informed the auction would begin in an hour. Cat asked the Romanian that seemed to speak the best English where the bathroom might be. He said he would take her. He walked her through the curtains and escorted her to a toilet and sink mounted to a wall. No door, no curtain, nada. She looked at the toilet, looked at the Romanian, and said, "Fine. Could you at least turn around?"

He looked at her and smiled. "Of course, miss."

Cat was not particularly bashful, so she dropped her jeans and underwear and sat down to do her business. She had a small pack of Kleenex in her purse, which she carried any time she left the country. You just never knew. She reached in her purse for a tissue.

She was feeling cramps coming on. Maybe that was one reason she had an overwhelming desire to kill Tim.

As she scrounged around her purse, she started to check her phone and remembered it had been taken. There was something strange. There was a calculator in her purse, something she never carried. Also, it was a ten dollar el-cheapo job. She used an H.P. scientific calculator. Being curious, she pulled the back off as she sat there. There was an extra battery. The printed circuit board did not look right. She would bet almost anything, at some point, Tim or someone with the Agency had slipped it into her purse. She would also bet double or nothing it was a GPS tracker of some sort. *Fucking bastards,* she thought. On the one hand, it pissed her off. On the other hand, she could understand that the tracker might just be a method for someone to see where she was. That could potentially be a lifesaver.

She finished her business at the toilet. Her escort accompanied her back to Tim. They sat in cheap folding chairs waiting for the auction to begin.

Knowing that the torpedo was the real deal, she suspected that Tim had an unlimited budget once the bidding began. The Romanians running the bid did their best to make the auction appear to have a certain element of "class." The bidders were served champagne and some sort of local alcoholic beverage called tuică. Cat had one. It was something like moonshine and had a similar kick. She was glad she quit at one.

One point three million dollars later, she and "Tim" were declared the winners. All seemed well, at first. A laptop was brought to Tim, and he used it to log into an account and authorize the deposit into the Romanians' Zurich account. By now, all the other bidders had left. That was when it all went south. Tim was elated while Cat was still suspicious.

The Romanians, smiling the entire time, invited Tim and Cat into a limo. After a ten-minute drive, they were escorted from the limo through an empty storefront into a small room with one door and no windows and locked inside. They were prisoners.

Tim seemed shocked, Cat, not so much. Tim paced back and forth expressing disbelief while Cat sat in a cheap metal chair listening to his rants. Then it got seriously bad. Scruffy-looking men opened their cell and brought the two of them into a large room.

"What the hell is up here?" Tim asked. "We've met all your conditions."

The Romanian that seemed to be the best English speaker laughed. "Thank you for the money. I would tell you to tell your CIA bosses we are not as stupid as they think, but you two will never speak to your bosses again. We appreciate the money, but someone else will actually get the weapon. There is a saying in this part of the world. There are only two commodities, gold and lead. Now that we have the gold, you two will see the lead."

Cat stood silently. To her surprise, her partner folded, totally.

"Look, there has to be another way. Let me leave. You can have the woman. I'm sure she would be valuable to someone..."

That was when the situation changed. The lights went out in the room, and red beams panned around, settling on Romanians. The "bad guys" dropped like flies. Cat heard popping sounds, smelled gunpowder, and actually heard a bullet impact the skull of the Romanian standing next to her. She smelled the copperish odor of blood.

The lights came back on. Four men dressed in black and holding wicked-looking guns with large tubes on the business end and red laser sights had appeared. The men's faces were obscured with balaclavas, and night vision glasses were flipped up on their helmets. The tallest man looked over the scene. Cat was standing. Dead Romanians littered the floor, and Tim was with them, lying in the fetal position.

"You two need to come with us," the tall man said quietly, mostly to Cat since Tim was just beginning to pick himself up from the floor.

"Do I have to ride with him?" she asked, pointing at Tim.

"Yeah, we heard him try to trade you for his freedom. Real piece of work. No, you don't have to ride with a coward. Can't say I blame you."

Tim seemed to grow a set. "I'm CIA. You guys work for us. Besides, I heard that, and you can't talk about me like that."

The man in black turned to Tim, smiled, and delivered a hard punch to his stomach. Tim issued an "oof" sound and dropped to his knees.

"I'm not CIA. I'm here to rescue your sorry ass and secure the weapon. I'll talk about your wimp ass any way I choose." Turning to Cat, he spoke in a much quieter and entirely different tone of voice. "Come with me, Miss King."

Thus C.A. King met John Black. The mission wasn't over of course. John and three of his men had come to rescue Cat and Tim. The remainder of John's squad had taken down the remaining Romanians guarding the torpedo and loaded it in a truck, which they had stolen earlier.

Only an hour had passed from the time Black made his entry into that room, guns blazing, until the entire group was aboard a Sikorsky CH-53 headed across the Black Sea toward Turkey.

Tim, being Tim, had been unable to leave well enough alone. He had verbally harassed Cat and John until John had finally placed the business end of a menacing-looking pistol to the center of Tim's forehead. He told him to sit down, shut up, and especially to stay as far away from Miss King as the interior of the helicopter allowed.

Tim got the message, but Cat found out later Tim was the son of someone important. Charges of some sort were soon brought against Cat and John Black. Cat's problems never even got past the paperwork stage. To start, she was a contract employee and had done everything exactly as instructed.

The CIA apparently was not totally inept and had eventually decided Tim was not operational material. The only downside was that Tim's relatives had pushed the Navy until they entered a fairly stern letter in Black's file. Blackie, being Blackie, had simply resigned his commission and walked away.

Realizing a mistake had been made, the Navy tried for some time to figure out some course that allowed everyone to save face. They even sent a high-ranking officer of some sort to Cat's condo to ask her to try to persuade John all was forgiven.

The officer had expressed the value SEALs had for John, for the nation as a whole. After fifteen minutes, he left with a promise from Cat that she would at least try. The officer left her with several means of contact for Black.

Cat considered the proposition after the officer left. She could see how Black could potentially be valuable to his squad and the country. She also had picked up on the fact that John Black was brash and bold, brilliant and rude, and a man who seemed to be able to give off an egotistical impression with a minimum of words. He could also be quite charming. She decided to accept the challenge.

Several calls and e-mails later, the two met for coffee, then drinks, and finally a weekend. After all that, she decided her initial impressions of John Fucking Black had been entirely correct on all counts. He seemed to her like a delicious entrée. One that was so high in calories that the guilt began with the first bite. John would be a fond memory to her and nothing more.

As it turned out, The Navy SEALs survived without John. He found other employment with the government that was still valuable to the national interests, and he and Cat never saw each other again.

Until this mission.

Chapter 35

Onboard Salvage One

Dawn

The sun crept out of the gray seas in the east. The entire scene was somewhat surreal. Cat and Ragan sat fifty feet away from John Black and a bomb capable of destroying a city, calmly smoking and sipping coffee. Black had ignored repeated requests to come out for a break.

Cat watched him now, the harsh lights from the portable light tower glaring on him even as the skies showed pink at the horizon, slowly chasing the darkness away. She could tell he was very close to finished. She also knew he had probably absorbed as much radioactive energy as a thousand chest x-rays.

She studied John closely. He tossed a tool back into the toolbox and peeled off his rubber gloves. He stood, very, very slowly, and turned toward her.

"I'm done," he announced, just before he collapsed to the steel deck.

Cat tugged on Ragan and ran to John. She rolled him over to his back. *Oh God, he's so pale.* "John, what's happened?"

"I'd say the clots have let go."

Ragan took one look at John and took off running, yelling into his radio for medical assistance as he ran.

John looked at Cat and smiled. "Glad he's gone. Gives us a little time."

"John, we'll get medics here. Everything will be okay." Tears began to flow. She felt tightness in her chest as panic set in.

"You're kidding yourself. We both know better. Listen closely, I may not have a chance to repeat this. One message for Ragan. I want a burial at sea, right here. SEALs in charge."

"Okay." She sobbed. "What else, asshole?"

"Once you're done with this one, walk away, Cat. The Agency will chew you up and spit you out sooner or later. People are nothing but assets to them. Walk away. Last, you and Mac, read the letters I left."

"Yes, sir," she mocked, saluting. "Anything else?"

"How 'bout a hug? I feel so cold..."

She didn't have anything smart to say, so she simply cradled his head in her arms and held him. As noisy and obnoxious as John Black had been in life, he was anything but in death. She knew he was gone but refused to admit it at that moment. Cat heard footsteps behind her, and she turned away from Black to see Ragan and two medical techs. She backed away as the techs knelt by John.

In just a moment one stood and turned to Cat. "I'm sorry, ma'am, but he's gone. Nothing we could do. He bled out internally."

Cat sat down next to John and held his hand. She looked at the tech and quietly said, "Thank you. You guys have performed a miracle keeping him alive this long."

The techs nodded, stood, and collected their gear. They had begun to leave when one turned. "Ma'am, if it matters, I believe he wasn't in pain at the end. The guys I know that almost bought it like that said they got cold and fell asleep." He turned and left.

"Miss King, I, uhm, I..."

"Don't worry Lieutenant. I know all you spec ops guys are super macho, but at this particular moment, you feel obligated to say something comforting to me. It's fine, I understand. This is all you need to know, all you need to do. Blackie wanted to be buried at sea, by SEALs, right here. That's all he asked of you, and you will do exactly that, or you will be dealing with one very pissed-off woman."

Ragan helped her up. "Yes, ma'am. I understand. It would be very wrong to not grant a dying man's last request, don't you think?"

They looked at each other. At this moment, they shared obligations to a dead man, each with their own burden but a shared sense of duty.

"Let me get you back to *Atlantis* while we get things under control here."

"I need to be present for John's burial. How long will it take to organize everything?"

"I'm sure he'd want it done on *Reuben James*, so I've got to see her C.O. It's really all up to him. His first priority is the weapon and *Salvage One* and her crew. I promise you this. There will be no burial at sea without you and Mac, so let's get you back to *Atlantis*. As soon as I've coordinated everything, you'll be the first to know. My guess is tomorrow."

"Thank you."

An hour later Cat was being lowered to the deck of *Atlantis* from *Reuben James'* helo. She waited for the tools to come down on the rope line and then turned away. She could see the questions on Mac's face.

He waited until the helicopter was far enough away to be able to talk. "Where's John?"

"I'm sorry, I thought you might have been told. He's dead. Right after he finished safeing the bomb, he collapsed. A few minutes later, he was gone."

Mac looked down. "No, I hadn't heard. Did he say anything?"

"Yes. He said a couple things. He wanted to be buried at sea, here, by SEALs, and he left envelopes for the two of us here on *Atlantis*. They seemed important to him."

Mac hugged Cat. It was a gesture that Cat could tell was not customary for Mac. In truth, it was not customary for Cat either. For a brief, private moment, the two shared their sense of loss.

"Ragan says he'll get with the captain of *Reuben James* to coordinate the ceremony. There are some operational things that will come first, but he'll contact me once a time is set. He said probably tomorrow."

"Yes, I can see that. *Atlantis* is in serious need of replenishment, but another twenty-four hours won't matter. Are you sure it's safe to close on the salvage ship?"

"Yes, I'm sure. John was very thorough."

"Okay. We're about thirty miles away, but I'll make sure we close up with *Reuben James*."

"Thank you, Mac. I know you and I will want to be there for the service."

"Yes, of course. What are your plans?"

"Honestly, a shower and a few hours of sleep. I think it's been at least two days since I slept, and I'm sure you're in the same shape. But the envelopes John left for us are my priority right now."

Mac nodded. "Agreed, let's go to his cabin. I'm sure his roommate is busy."

"Do you have a key?"

"Actually yes. John gave me one right after we left Woods Hole. Strange…"

The two left the stern work area and headed for John's cabin. "Not so strange. John was dying of pancreatic cancer. Did he tell you?"

"No, that sucks, but it explains a lot now that I think about it. He's been an entirely different John, wouldn't you agree? I mean, since you two were acquainted and all…"

She shook her head. "That's not fair, not at all. Yes, we probably should have told you, but would it have really made a difference for this mission?"

She could tell he was considering that thought as they went below, negotiating the corridors, headed for the chief engineer's cabin that Black had shared. "No, you're right. I don't see how I would have done anything differently. The question might be, would you and John have done anything differently?"

"Fair enough. Honestly, I couldn't say. So, I guess we just put that behind us?"

"Agreed." Mac knocked, waited a moment, and opened the door. It was a typical cabin with bunk beds on one side and a desk and two lockers on the opposite side. Cat was mildly surprised to find the cabin very neat and clean. There were a few pictures on the desk of the chief engineer with his wife and kids. A few novels were on a wall-mounted bookshelf. There wasn't a sign of anything in the cabin that looked like it might have been John's.

Mac went to the locker labelled "JFB." Searching through a large key ring, he found the appropriate key and opened the locker.

He and Cat were both surprised, sort of, at the weapons cache in the locker. She saw two submachine guns of unknown varieties, a grenade launcher, and a very short-barreled shotgun she was fairly confident was illegal in all fifty states.

Mac looked on the shelf above the armory. Sure enough, there were two envelopes. Picking them up, he handed one to Cat. "Miss King, I'd assume John would want us to read these in private. This one is yours."

Taking the envelope simply labelled "Cat," she nodded, gave Mac a hug, and headed for her cabin. A short walk down the hall and up a steep stairway brought her to the room she shared with another tech. She knocked and, hearing no answer, entered. It seemed oddly funny somehow that the cabin she and her roommate occupied was really not terribly different from John's. If anything, it was a little less organized.

She desperately wanted a shower and a nap, but there was absolutely no way John's letter wasn't coming first. Sitting on the lower bunk, she opened the envelope. She saw John's strange mixture of printing and cursive. He had some of the neatest handwriting for a man she had ever seen, even allowing for the fact that many technical types tended to write in a neat, clear fashion.

Cat – If you're reading this, I suppose we can assume I'm quite dead. I had a few things I wanted you to know, about me, and us, and perhaps about you.

Unless I've met my end in some other way, pancreatic cancer has probably taken me. You probably are sad, at least I think I hope you are. Don't be. I've lived an incredibly full life, and I've done it pretty much how I chose to.

Do I have regrets? Hell yes. One is my wife. She deserved a better, less selfish and self-absorbed man. Another is you. I never shared my feelings for you. There were, what I thought, good reasons. You were (and are) way too young for me. You're a much kinder and caring person. We are nothing alike, and yet, in some ways, we were very much alike.

We understood each other. We have a hard time dealing with fools. We demand that people around us do their jobs to the best of their ability. But we both know, as much as it will always pain me, we couldn't have been a couple.

My dear Cat, I have to close. Don't mourn me. Find something pleasant in your memory we did and remember that. Do NOT stay with the Agency. And if possible, go to work for Mac. He's a fine man and a fair man. He could use someone like you.

With as much love as I'm capable of feeling – John

She smiled, weeping at the same time. She carefully folded the letter and placed it in her personal drawer. It was time for a shower. And sleep.

Chapter 36

Aboard the Rueben James
Near sunset, the next day

It was raining, fitting weather for a funeral. It was also another reminder that summer was at end in the North Atlantic. Because of the weather, the skipper of *Reuben James* had moved the ceremony to the helicopter hangar after having the helo moved out to the landing deck.

The funeral was very short. Apparently, that was the way of the SEALs. The ship's chaplain spoke briefly. Lt. Ragan asked if Mac or Cat wanted to speak. Cat wasn't able. She thought Mac did a wonderful, and brief, job. He told the few people present how long he and John had been friends, that John was a hero, and that he was the most irritating asshole he had ever had the honor of meeting.

Mac sat down with Cat. She leaned over. "Wonderful job, Mac. I see why John thought so much of you." She thought Mac looked sharp. He had worn his old chief's uniform, and it still fit him well. She looked around. Ragan's men must have borrowed some more appropriate uniforms from the ship to replace their combat gear. Cat wore her best jeans and a Woods Hole windbreaker.

The ship's crew had supplied men from their security detail to have enough manpower for the actual act of committing John to the deep. In addition, there had been about forty crewmembers that attended just to say goodbye to a former Navy veteran.

When the speaking portion of the ceremony ended, John's body, in its weighted bag, was moved to the edge of the deck and covered with a flag. The small crowd followed.

Each of the four SEALs onboard *Reuben James* filed up to the body. One at a time, each man pulled something from a pocket and placed it inside the bag.

"What are they doing?" Cat whispered to Mac.

"Each SEAL is placing one of his gold trident SEAL emblems in the bag with the body. In a burial on land, they would file by and pound the pin into the top of the casket with their fist."

"And the meaning?"

"It's a custom. Not being a SEAL, I suspect it's a way of saying your brothers will always be with you, even in death."

"I understand, I think."

Ragan's four men, and two more from the ship, took up positions holding a flag flat over the body in its bag. Taps was played over the ship's PA system, and the chaplain said a few words about committing John's body to the deep until it was called up by God in the end times. With the wind and rain, Cat really couldn't hear every word.

With that, two men tilted the board John's bagged body rested on as Ragan and his SEALs held the United States flag over the body. Once the board had tilted enough, Mac and Cat's friend slid into the Atlantic Ocean. They walked back into the helicopter hangar to get out of the rain.

Two or three minutes later, Ragan showed up.

"Thank you, Lieutenant, you and your men did a wonderful job," Mac said as he shook Ragan's hand.

Cat shook Ragan's hand as well. "I'm sure John appreciates you sending him off." She was sure she probably looked odd to Ragan because she could feel a tear trickling down her cheek even as she forced a smile. Then again, maybe it was just the rain.

"If you two have just a few minutes, the skipper has some papers for you. It's customary for the captain of the ship to fill out a certificate for any burial at sea. It lists name and rank of the deceased and the time, date, and lat and lon of the burial. Normally it's sent to the next of kin. The legend that follows John around said all he has is an ex and the two don't speak. I asked the skipper to fill out three, one for each of you and one to hold in case a relative shows up."

"Thanks, Lieutenant, that's very thoughtful of you," Mac said as Cat nodded.

Ragan walked away, leaving the two alone in the hangar.

"I suppose you read John's letter?" Mac asked.

"Yes, actually it was personal. I suppose I'm glad he did it. It cleared up some stuff between the two of us. What about yours?"

"The same I suppose. But there were some items in it that needed to be passed on relating to how the bad guys may have found out about the weapons in the first place. I sent an e-mail last night passing that information along to the appropriate parties."

"Good. I don't know who they are, but there should be a price to be paid."

Onboard Atlantis
Two hours later

Cat and John sat in the wardroom having dinner. The canned soup helped remind them how low the ship was on provisions.

"By morning we should be docking in Greenland. We'll refuel, re-provision, and head back."

"I hope our spare parts show up. We may not have a lot of time left before the pingers in the black boxes quit." Cat was obviously concerned about getting her sonar gear back up and running. A replacement for Homer was supposed to be waiting for them as well.

"You're right. By the way, Ragan and his people are back aboard the *Alabama*. It surfaced long enough to pick them up and is off to the next hot spot."

"Good thing they got here when they did."

"Absolutely. Earlier would have been even better. The thing is, though, Karen would have done something at some point to try to scuttle the mission."

"I suppose. I didn't know her, did you?"

"No, she was a last-minute addition. Either way, though, she slipped through background checks somehow. That's being looked into as well. Oh, one other thing. By the time we can get back on station, there should be a Norwegian research vessel and a British Navy ship joining the search. Our Navy has a salvage ship standing by in Boston as well."

"I hope we can get the airliner located. A lot of families need closure." She stood. "More coffee?"

"Of course. Thank you."

She re-filled both of their cups and leaned back in her chair. Mac did the same. The room became silent for a few minutes.

"Mac, I want you to know I'm not going to be working for the Agency any more. John made a point of telling me that in his letter. Would this be a bad time to ask about working with you?"

"No, in fact it's a very good time. We'll make arrangements as soon as we get back."

"Thank you, I look forward to being a permanent associate of yours."

Mac nodded, smiled, and gently punched her in the shoulder.

Chapter 37

It was dark as coal in the high desert. The five man CIA black team headed up the gravel road toward the cabin. There was no moon. The stars were so bright the men could probably have seen quite well without their night vision goggles. As they approached the cabin, it was obvious the wind was absolutely calm. The smoke rose in a nearly straight line from the chimney.

The team had interrupted the power where it left the county road several hundred yards from the cabin. The telephone service had been carefully interrupted as well. When the team departed, everything would be restored, down to resetting clocks. Even the VCR that constantly flashed 12:00 would show the correct time for the only time in its life.

The Agency had sent a black team with the mission to take one Martin Parks, U. S. Air Force (ret), into custody for interrogation and then to terminate him. The simple reason for the black team was that, by law, the CIA had absolutely no jurisdiction inside the United States. That was the red line that separated them from the FBI.

Unfortunately, Parks was believed to have been in contact with individuals outside the United States, which *were* within the scope of the Agency. Besides, the people in Langley had no trust or respect for anyone other than themselves. Even that was hardly considered to be a one hundred percent guarantee of purity of heart and mind. So, an illegal kidnapping and termination of a retired Air Force officer had been actively underway for about thirty minutes.

As the group approached the cabin, the team leader gestured to two men to proceed ahead. One went to the front and another to the back of the small but beautiful cabin. Each was equipped with a very sensitive microphone and a periscope camera to look and listen inside. The intent was to verify Parks was alone.

One came back to the team leader after three minutes. "Something strange inside, sir."

"What?"

"Well, the subject's computer is on. Monitor is lit up like a searchlight, and, well, I'd say Mr. Parks ate his gun."

"Okay, must have a battery backup on the computer." The team leader waited a few minutes until the man assigned to the rear of the cabin arrived. "Do either of you see any indication of alarms or surveillance cameras?"

Both replied in the negative. "Okay, we'll make class I entry." In English, that meant the team would pick a lock, wherever was easiest and most practical.

The team looked at the team leader. One member asked the important question. "Sterile entry, sir?"

That translated to booties and gloves. "Negative. If Mr. Parks is already dead of a self-inflicted GSW, no need for sterile entry. We'll set up a fire when we exit. No need for them to find Parks a week from now when he stinks. We gather what we need and burn it down. Evans, get us inside."

Three minutes later, the team was inside. The computer tech approached the team leader while the rest of the team was searching the cabin. "Sir, you need to see this."

The team leader walked into the room holding the computer and desk.

"Sir, the last email on the computer might have led to the suicide. There's also a response."

The team leader looked at the primitive AOL screen still displayed.

> *JFB: Parks, Martin*
> *Your actions have caused good people to die. Thankfully you didn't kill millions. I trusted you asshole. JFB*
> There was a reply.
> *Parks, Martin: JFB*
> *I'm sorry*

"What do you think, sir?"

"Looks like a suicide note to me. Mirror the hard drive. Look for any storage material of any kind, floppies, whatever, and take it with us. TEN MINUTES, EVERYONE!" he shouted.

Since Martin Parks was deceased, there would be no interrogation, nor would there be any need to terminate him. Instead, the black team's task would now be to gather any information and evidence that could be grabbed in the next ten minutes or so.

The team leader watched as one of his men pulled the hard drive from Park's computer, connected a wiring harness to it, and copied everything from one drive to the other. The computer's drive was replaced. Four men were combing the cabin end to end, top to bottom.

"Okay, let's go. Set up a gas explosion and we're out of here. Go!"

Three minutes later the team assembled on the porch. The team leader spoke into a hand-held radio. "Ready for pickup in ten at the drive, copy?"

"Copy," a disembodied voice answered.

Ten minutes later, as the black team headed down the county road in a dusty AT&T van, an orange flash appeared in the distance.

Chapter 38

Aboard Atlantis

0630 hrs local time

Two days later

Mac and Cat sat alone in the wardroom drinking coffee and picking at their breakfast.

"Here," Mac announced, rolling out a chart on the table. "This will be our search area. The overall search radius has been widened. Each of the three vessels has their own area."

Cat studied the chart. "Is there any significance to us having this particular area?"

Mac smiled. "Of course. I chose this one because it contains most of John's original guestimate."

"And?"

"And we'll pass right by Homer's last known location."

"I'm glad. He's a good ROV. I've become attached to the little robot. Not that his backup is incapable. I'm a little surprised Woods Hole was able to get all the parts to us we asked for. It'll be nice to have fresh groceries as well."

"Amen. Glad they shipped some food items from home as well. I've never been especially fond of the local fare in Greenland."

"Yeah, pickled fish and seal soup aren't very high on my list either. Give me yogurt, oatmeal, and a scrambled egg any day. Hell, Raisin Bran beats most Scandinavian food."

"You aren't eating much. Is everything okay?"

"Just missing John here at the table plotting and scheming with us."

"As do I. We go back a long way." Mac picked at his breakfast as well.

Atlantis went through a long, corkscrew roll where she pitched in two axis at one. That happened when a ship crossed a large wave quartering rather than head-on. In the two days they had been in port re-provisioning, a low-pressure front had moved in. In all likelihood, one would follow another all through the fall and into the winter. The North Atlantic was not a pleasant place to be in the winter.

"Is this normal?" Cat asked.

"Afraid so," Mac replied. "Actually, it'll probably get worse. I hope we can find the wreck soon."

"It's going to be really hard to find the black boxes with *Atlantis* moving around like this. I'm glad the Navy salvage ship will actually recover them. Evan's really, really good, but I'll predict you'll see sweat popping up on his forehead as he works the joysticks."

"Have you trained a new camera operator yet?"

"Sort of. Evan tells me one of the repair techs named Connie is familiar with the equipment, just not the actual job, but we'll manage."

"We'll be on site just after dinner I would guess."

"I should go below and finish our power-up checks I suppose. Mac, what's going to happen to the crew of *Salvage One*?"

"I honestly don't know. I would suspect you can get more information from your friends at the Agency than I've heard from my contacts."

"No, not a word, which somehow assures me they're busy figuring out how to hide all this. They just have no need for me anymore." Cat stood, placed her dishes in the used container, and headed out the door. "I'll be in my cave if you need me."

"Thanks. You know, I'm glad to have worked with you, Miss King."

"Same here." She smiled and walked away.

Mac sipped his coffee and thought. He had followed up on the tips Blackie had left him regarding the possible source of the leak about the weapons. A short and simple email to an old friend in the Office of Naval Intelligence was the extent of Mac's involvement, but he was quite sure there had been a response.

Cat was concerned about *Salvage One*'s crew. He suspected he knew why and probably shared her concerns. Yes, there were definitely evil people aboard the ship; however, there were also people who were simply the people who allowed any ship to function. Cooks, engineers, electricians, and many others who doubtless had no clue about the ship's mission. Those sailors likely held little or no political affiliation either.

Piracy was serious business. International law was involved. In this case, though, huge mistakes had been made by people in authority in the United States, mistakes that could have potentially resulted in thousands, maybe even millions, of deaths. Mac had absolutely no doubt that people in the States were scrambling right now to keep those mistakes from ever seeing the light of day.

He mentally went down a list of people on *Atlantis* that actually knew enough to be a threat to keeping all this secret. The list wasn't long, but he had serious concerns about what lengths the government would go to in order to contain the threat. Then it came to him in a flash. There was a way, and he would begin preparations to carry out his plan. If he was forced to do so, he would. Releasing the entire story would short-cut the lies and bullshit presently being concocted in Washington.

On the bridge – 1900 hrs

Mac sat in his chair, finally getting to spend some time with Clive Cussler. It was dark and cold outside the windows on the bridge, rain spat at the glass.

Atlantis struggled to maintain position on the surface as their ROV worked on the sea floor. Cat had requested, and Mac had consented to, trying to find Homer. Since Homer had been dragged when Atlantis ran, trying to escape being blown up by an accidental detonation of one of the bombs, his exact location had been an unknown.

Homer's umbilical cord had finally been cut, leaving about a mile of cable on the seafloor. Following the cable with the new ROV would lead directly to Homer. So, while Cat and her small crew in the conex container on the deck searched, Mac sat in his chair, reading his book and slowly rocking back and forth as *Atlantis* rolled in the eight-foot seas. His portable radio interrupted his reading.

"Mac, can you come to the trailer?"

Hmm, it never ends, does it? "I guess. Is it important? I'm just getting to the racy part in my book."

"I'll buy you a new one. Come on down."

"Okay, I'll be down in a few minutes." He folded the book's jacket into the page he was reading and shut the book. He set it on the dash below the window.

Turning to the helmsman, he said, "I'll be in the trailer. Try to keep everything as boring as possible."

"Will do, sir." The young man grinned.

Mac headed off the bridge, headed for the hallway and the stairs. He passed one of the side windows. Duct tape still covered the hole that had been left by one of the bullets fired by the SEALs to take down the pirates. He shook his head. There was a lot to be said for boring.

After a five-minute trek, he opened the door and entered the conex.

"Welcome to my lair, Captain sir!" Cat greeted him, smiling from ear to ear. "We have something to show you that will make you very happy, and it's all Connie's fault. Have a seat." She stood, urging Mac to sit in her comfortable office-style chair. The trailer was always the same. It was dimly lit to allow better views of the multiple monitors. The three people manning the board sat in front of the long array of screens, dials, and controls. It was all very space-ship looking to Mac, or anyone not familiar with the equipment.

"So, what is it that will make me happy, and why is Connie responsible?"

Cat turned to her ROV pilot. "Evan, recreate what happened from the tape for Captain MacAdams."

He nodded. "Okay, sir, watch these two monitors. The left one is the view from the camera, and the right one is the display from the sonar. So, as you can see, we had the cable in sight and were following it."

"So you found Homer?"

"No. Not yet, but we will. Homer is at the end of this cable. Go on, Evan," Cat responded, gently patting Mac on the shoulder as she stood behind him.

"So, Connie was looking at the controls for the sonar and asked me what the plane switch did. I explained we could look at the sonar images in either the horizontal plane, which was customary, or the vertical plane. Anyway, I switched it to vertical to humor her, and we were following the cable, and then Connie noticed the anomaly."

"Anomaly. That's a fancy word for something strange, right?"

"Absolutely. But the thing was, what Connie thought was strange really wasn't...Aw heck. Just watch the sonar picture, and I'll explain. There, do you see it?"

"Yes, that part of the return went blank. What causes that?"

Cat took up the narration. "We explained to Connie the display went blank because the sonar had no return, and that was because there was a canyon there. So, I told Evan to break off following the cable and mosey on over to the canyon just to satisfy Connie's curiosity."

"But why didn't we know about this canyon to begin with?"

"We probably would have, eventually. The canyon was two to three hundred meters outside our original search area. I'm sure we'd have got to it sooner or later. Other stuff came up..."

"Yeah, for sure. So, what happened that's going to make me very happy?"

"Watch this," Evan said as he resumed playing the recorded view. The camera followed the muddy ocean floor, seemingly ten or so feet off the bottom. The bottom began to gradually fall away. "This area is what Connie noticed. The bottom is dropping at about the same angle as the sonar takes on leaving the ROV, so the return disappears. Voilà, a blank spot on the display."

"So that's what Connie saw?"

"Yes, sir." Connie finally spoke up. She looked to be mid-twenties and had a slightly tomboy look to her. She looked and sounded rather shy. Had the lighting been better, Mac was pretty sure he would have seen her blushing. "It seemed odd to me that part of the screen was just blank. It was quite normal to these two, but all new to me. The good thing is that they humored me."

"Wow!" Mac was looking as the video showed a black chasm appearing. The camera's view panned down, following a slope of over forty-five degrees.

"Now, watch this," Evan said quietly.

Suddenly Mac could see a flash of white and a straight line. The camera view changed. Evan had moved the ROV and then panned back over. Mac gasped. He was looking right at it. The tail of an airplane. Right in front of him. UNITED AIRLINES painted on it. "Well, I'll be damned."

"Here's the live picture," Evan told him, flipping a few switches. "It looks like we've got about a twenty-foot-long segment of fuselage with part of the tail attached."

"The good news is that's also the segment that has the data and voice recorders in it," Cat announced proudly.

"So, we have the black boxes."

"Yep. We've got them, Mac."

"The canyon, does it explain why we couldn't hear the pingers?"

"Yes. You'd have to be right on top to hear them."

"So, where do you think the rest of the plane is?"

"Can't say, but I think when we ship photos of the edges where the tail broke away from the rest of the plane, the experts may be able to tell when the tail separated. If it was when the plane hit the water, the rest of the wreckage might be very close. If the tail came off at thirty thousand feet, the wreckage could be miles away."

Mac nodded. "Yes, I was thinking along the same lines. Congratulations, all of you. It would seem *Atlantis* has an e-mail to send out. Miss King, would you like to help me draft it?"

"Of course."

CNN has learned that the research vessel Atlantis *out of the Oceanographic Institute at Woods Hole has announced that the tail section of United Airlines flight 92 has been located. Experts say this is the same section of the airplane where the black boxes are located. There are two other vessels involved in the search, and predictions are that it is possible other portions of the wreckage may be located soon.*

In other news, a State Department official has announced eleven men have been taken into custody in Greenland and will be charged with piracy on the high seas. There were no other details given. We'll relate details to you as they become available.

Epilogue

On the Pakistan/Afghan Border

Bin Ladin and his science advisor sat in the cave. The science advisor turned off the tape recorder, removed the cassette, and handed it to Bin Ladin.

The two sipped their tea, and Bin Ladin stroked his beard. The science advisor finally broke the silence.

"There are very few details, but it would seem our efforts to obtain the atomic bombs from the infidels has met with failure."

"What *do* we know?"

"We know the submarine disappeared, the salvage vessel was damaged, and it has been seized and taken to Greenland. Some of the crew is in custody."

"There is no possibility to trace any of this back to us?"

"No. It will hardly be a secret to the intelligence agencies in the West that what they call terrorists were behind this, but that will be all. There are several layers between us and the people in custody."

Bin Laden nodded. "Very well."

There was a long silence in the room.

"What do we do now?"

"We continue the fight. After all, time is on our side."

The End

Other Books by Donald Churchwell

All books are available on Amazon.

Please visit my Facebook page;
donaldchurchwellbooks

About the Author

Donald lives a quiet life in North Florida with his wife. They both have "real" jobs, a grown daughter, and grandchildren. As a mystery writer, he feels some mystery about the author is a good thing. Besides, your concept of what he's like could be a lot more exciting than the reality.

If you feel you simply must know more about the author, please visit Donald Churchwell Books on Facebook. Roam around, "like" the page. You will get updates on works in progress, and you'll be the first to know when something new is coming out.

One more thing. Donald wanted to share what he *isn't*. He's not an ex-SEAL, Ranger, Marine Recon, or any of that really cool stuff. Nor did he ever work for one of those alphabet agencies. So anything you read as he weaves his fictional characters through history is just the product of an overactive imagination and too much caffeine and could never have *really* happened. Honest.

Acknowledgements

This one was fun to write. The idea for it actually came to me a few years ago. I was in a hotel in Portland, Oregon to attend my nephew's wedding. A Malaysian Airlines airliner had gone missing after leaving Malaysia. I wondered what could possibly be found instead of an airliner in a deep-sea search. I wrote the idea down in the book I keep with me.

I had two other books in progress, but slowly added details as they came to me.

As luck would have it, while I worked on the outline, I managed to accidently find an ex B-52 pilot (thanks Gary!) as well as an expert on SEAL and deep-sea work with ROV's that needs to remain nameless.

So, given all that, thanks to them and the usual suspects. Devin for editing, Alexis for another stunning cover, Tomi for formatting, and my wife for just putting up with my crap. Thank you all!!

And thanks to my readers for being patient.

Made in the USA
Columbia, SC
10 August 2020